I0459236

# Never Marry A Warlock

## Omnibus Edition

By

Marilyn Vix

Shadowcat Publishing

San Jose, California

Format: Omnibus Edition

Author: Marilyn Vix

Cover Design: Melody Simmons of eBookindiecovers

Editor: Shelley Holloway, hollowayhouse.me

ISBN: **0692692517**
ISBN-13: **978-0692692516**

"*Never Marry a Warlock* is a novella that combines competent eroticism, humor, and rapid-fire pacing."

~IndieReader 12/26/13

"Vix's style lends itself well to the ratcheted pace, and is very conversational — there is no getting bogged down by purple prose or evidence of an author so enamored with her own words that she meanders. Vix does *not* meander. Her characters are a lot of fun, and it's hard not to like Cat right from the start, especially with Vix's sharp wit and humor that kept me snickering as I turned the pages."

~by S. N. Graves at Disturbed Graves Blog<br>Oct. 29, 2014

"This was such a quick fun read. It was hilarious, and sometimes heartbreaking. And yet it's also pretty steamy. There's some great plot twists that had me shocked."

~Reviewed by Maghon Thomas at Happy Tails and Tales Blog 11/2/15

Marilyn Vix writes fast paced paranormal romances with strong females finding their HEA with hot warlocks, vampires, and time travelers. She currently lives in Northern California with her husband. This is her first novella series.

Marilyn is currently working on her first full-length novel, *Everything For Love*. For more information about her books, visit her website at: marilynvix.com.

To my husband
You're my pillar

# CONTENTS

## Never Marry A Warlock

## Never Fall For A Warlock

## Never Cross A Warlock

# Never Marry A Warlock

Beware of Warlocks, Book 1

# Chapter 1

My husband's arms were wrapped around her naked body. The blankets were strewn and interwoven between their legs. He was spooning her with his biceps draped over her. I stood in the doorway taking in the scene of my husband and my best friend. It was the end of the world, at least for me. But I wasn't going to take it lying down. I should have known better than to have married a warlock.

I hit him with a force spell that knocked him up against the headboard. He fell back down and braced his hands out to catch his fall. Cassandra scrambled out of the bed, dragging the silk comforter with her. Bitch. She better get out of my way. She was next.

Rich was naked as he sat up to look at me. Normally, the abs-flash trick would work. But not now. I was too pissed off. I knew what spells he used to look like that. It was easy to fool a mortal and ex-best friend on the floor. But not me. Thing is, we were too evenly matched. I think that was the problem.

He threw a counter spell that lanced light through my arm, digging into the flesh as it tried to anchor and link me to him. I flicked out a removal spell that broke the connection, laced my hands together, and hit him with a burst of everything I had. He went flying backward, through the window into the pool. It was satisfying to watch. He tried to rise up and hover toward me, but I knocked him back in the water with another force spell.

He yelled from the pool. His wavy, brown hair trenched with water. "Baby, we can talk it out. It's just a moment of weakness. You've had them with mortals."

I'd drown him if he couldn't breathe water. Blowing up the six-million-dollar house probably wouldn't kill him either. Like I said, never marry a warlock. I shot another burst of energy, creating a field that pushed him under. He swam back up and came to the side, with both chiselled arms on the edge of the pool. His brown eyes tried to melt my insides. I wasn't going to let him win again.

I walked through the window ledge, broken glass crackling under my heels. "It's over Rich. Just over. I'm done with playing the games, or sharing you with the next mortal you pick up. Really, when I said my vows, it was forsaking everyone. Including mortals."

"I haven't touched another witch in ages, Catherine. Really. Scout's honor."

I blasted him into the pool again. Rich came up from the bottom, laughing. He swam back to the side and got out. He walked toward me with glistening, rock-hard muscles. I fought down the attraction, along with the writhing anger. Maybe blowing him up was too good for him. Slow, painful death. Maybe.

He walked up to me, his brown hair wet and slicked back, brown eyes mirroring the puppy I had as a kid. "It's only good fun. Really, I haven't been with another witch the entire year of our marriage."

"Which is now over." I crossed my hands in finality. "I'm not renewing the yearly vow. It's done." With a final touch to his arm, I put a lock spell on him. He froze for a moment and grinned with a snarl. Rich vibrated and lines glowed on him as he tried to counter the spell.

I knew it wouldn't hold him for long. It was just my time to get away before he tried to kill me. Sweet-talking would only buy so much time before he'd retaliate. Like I said, we were evenly matched, and our marriage had been a good peace between us. Until now.

I raced through the room, past the ex-friend mortal cringing under the comforter on the floor. I yelled to her, "You're lucky I don't have time for you." I could see Cassandra's blonde hair and blue eyes as she brought the blanket down to get a better look at me. "How did you do that?" she whimpered from under her tent city.

"I'm a witch, you bitch." But then I felt Rich's energy building behind me, and knew I had to get out of there before he brought the house down on me. I ran down the hall through the broad mansion living room, knowing that all that decorating would be wasted now since I wasn't coming back. I'd had the crystal chandelier in the dining room imported from Prague. My handcrafted antique oak table would be splinters in moments. Damn, I'd miss that. I heard the click of my heels as I jammed across the marble front entryway and got through the front door.

My right heel slipped, but I kept my balance as I raced for my Jag. A lightning bolt shot through the house. I only had seconds to dodge or counter. I spun, faced the bolt aimed at me, and countered its direction. It split into several sparks that veered off in opposite directions. They ended in a shower of fireworks that would impress a small town on the Fourth of July.

I jumped in my burgundy Jaguar, got the engine running with a push of the button, and started down the main driveway before he could send another bolt. I knew the car could ground more bolts because of the spells I'd set on it. But a direct hit could fry the entire electrical system. The car was definitely worth more than the man right now.

I needed to get out of Rich's range. I floored it on the winding road, hearing a hiss and burst of dirt behind me. I knew he'd miss if I kept moving and got out of range in time. Zigzagging lightning on a winding road sucked for aiming. Thank the gods it was to my advantage right now.

I drove north along the coast until I couldn't hear any more blasts behind me. He was a sore loser, but he'd taken the last step in the wrong direction. Luckily, witches only married for a year. With renewals every anniversary, it could be annulled if not renewed at the vow date. This was one marriage I would be happy to walk away from.

I reminded myself never to marry a warlock again.

# Chapter 2

I floored the Jag. All I knew was that I was heading north. I could find another town, make another identity, and find another man. One tear started to well in my eye. I sniffed. No. I wasn't going to let Richard get to me. It was over. Anything had to be better. I would just head north. I'd find it along the way.

I pulled into a small beach town along Hwy 1. It was like the rest, with a diner, main market, and tourist trap shops that hawked knick-knacks with shells. I'd seen it a thousand times. I needed something more permanent. I saw the sign, "Firewater Bar." That would do. I needed something strong to dull the pain.

I sat at a stool and ordered a glass of port. At least the one thing about this part of California, right below Carmel, they usually stocked the good stuff of everything. Everyone from the very rich to sometimes famous could drop in without notice, and they usually had cash. I had at least the cash, and the will to forget. Too bad I had a witch's metabolism. I would have loved to get drunk. Except it would take ten times what it would take for a mortal. But no one ever would know that, unless you were one of us.

"How come a pretty lady like you is sitting alone?" It was some local at the other end of the bar. I swivelled on the barstool, not an easy thing to do in a white cotton knit dress. It clung around my legs, highlighting the tan I'd worked hard to develop by the pool. "Feeling like I need a shot. Would you like one?"

The guy got up and walked over to the stool next to me. "You look like you need me to buy you the drink. That bad huh?" Interesting, he actually sounded concerned.

I knocked the port back and signalled the bartender to load us both up again.

"Just caught my husband with another woman."

"Oh shit. That does sound like it's been a bad day." He slid down as he gave the bartender a look.

The bartender walked over between the mortal guy and me to pour my shot of port. He turned to the guy next to me. "The usual, Jed?"

The bartender pulled a bottle of bourbon from under the bar and refilled his glass. Jed took a drink and nodded to the bartender. "Thanks, Alan. You serve only the best."

I took a sip and sighed. "You're right, was it Jed?" The guy next to me nodded. "It just sucks." I took another sip of the port. I had to get a grip. But at least, if I said it out loud, it might help. I closed my eyes, still seeing Cassandra entwined in Rich's arms. "He was with my best friend."

Jed whistled in response. "Better make that a double for her, Alan. I'll catch the tab." He leaned into me. He seemed like an ordinary guy, complete with baseball cap, plaid shirt, and jeans. Not remarkable, but a solid ear to listen.

I snorted as I lifted my glass to clink with his. "It's been a shitty day. But I've got my health." I raised my glass after the bartender poured me another shot. At least, I had my hide, but I had one pissed off warlock that might be on my ass in a few hours. I'd eventually have to deal with him. But hell, it had been a bad day. I looked around at the cowboy décor of the bar. Willie Nelson was playing on the stereo in the background. Amazing what you miss when you're distracted by emotions.

"So," Jed said as the bartender walked away. He gave me an up and down look. "What kind of man would do that to a fine kind of lady like you? Is he nuts?"

I smiled. I'd like to wrap something around Rich's neck. I considered wrapping his nuts, but I knew they wouldn't be big enough. I tried to block the memory of Cassandra with him. I remember him doing the same thing to me. I closed my eyes. "Damn it, why does it have to hurt so much? We've only been together a year."

"Shit, that is rough. Cheating that early. You are better off without him." Jed put his hand on my shoulder.

I nodded and sipped my drink, the syrup texture glided down my throat. Something had to anchor me. I crossed my legs Maybe I just needed a completely new start. Maybe I needed a new face, town, and life.

"I think I need to start over."

"Amen to that." Jed concurred as he took a drink.

I took out a fifty and tossed it on the bar. "Give Jed another round on me, and you can keep the change, Alan."

Willie sang me out as I walked through the door, not looking back. I needed somewhere else to sort myself out. But where?

Anchored in the Jag, I felt more in control. The rhythm of the road turns gave me a sense of power and strength I'd lost over the last year. I felt stronger than I had in a long time. I was on my own again, and I liked it. The ocean breeze blasted through the window. The shore crept onward, guiding me north away from him, the past, everything.

I saw the turn off to Pacific Grove and took the exit. A good hotel, a night to rest, and cleaning up would be a good way to gain focus. I needed something to reset my inner compass. The ocean was always so cleansing. I picked a B&B near the shore. It was one of those Victorian restorations that always looked so quaint.

I parked the Jag and stepped out onto a gravel drive. I walked to the office door, smelling the fragrance of roses and rosemary. A cat lounged on one of the wicker chairs on the porch as I opened the screen door. I walked into a small reception area complete with wooden desk, old-fashioned key boxes, and Victorian ottoman. A tall man looked up and smiled. It was the only one I'd seen all day. I set my sunglasses on my head and smiled at the man behind the desk. "A room for one please."

A bath can do wonders. I slid down in the bubbles, letting the water slide over my body. The room came furnished in a rose motif with all the special touches you expect in a B&B. Candles dotted the bathroom with matching pink towels. The lavender bubble bath worked to relax my mind and muscles. However, the romantic feel was lost on me. The decorations of romantic bliss gave the illusion of comfort. Luckily, I did like pink. But having a room like this by myself was lonely.

I sighed as the lavender scent filled the bathroom. Stop it. I had to let go. Move on. I was better off without Rich. But the tears started, and I let them. One by one, they fell in the water, and I let the damn break inside me. Sobs echoed off the walls as I let it all out. It was enough to get by. Tomorrow had to be better. Jed was right. Today had totally sucked.

# Chapter 3

There is one thing I really love about Monterey and Pacific Grove: the shops. The boutiques are little worlds of shopping. Each is a place to get lost in new experiences. I needed to supplement my lack of wardrobe and toiletries. Soaps, shoes, skirts, and blouses, oh my.

I picked up some cute numbers. I especially loved a burgundy blouse and tight, leather mini skirt. I combined it all with some lovely black leather sandals. I got a couple of shorts, a set of dress pants and sweater, and a lovely silver lace bra. I even found a fabulous set of earrings and matching sea-glass necklace, all set with silver. I was ready for come what may. Plus, I was feeling a lot better. Nothing like a good shopping trip to make a girl feel whole again.

I changed into one of the blouses, a white and black floral print, and a cute pair of tight-fitting black cotton shorts. I picked up some tortoise shell-colored sunglasses with those big lenses for the movie star look. It made you look important when you walked into a room. I wanted to look fierce as I reclaimed my life. Mission accomplished with wardrobe replacement.

I let the road calm me as I continued north. Through the Bay Area, past Mendocino, and up through the coast past Fort Bragg, the scenery helped me forget. Rich was in the past now. The only course was forward. If that meant north, so be it.

I grew less worried of attack. I knew eventually he would find me. A battle was inevitable. We might clash causing a lot of physical scars, but he had caused some mental ones I needed to mend before we met again. Healing was more than just the physical. It was more of a soul issue. But I was looking forward to charring some pieces of him off. I was thinking of one specific part in fact. But that would be too easy. He'd probably guard it the most.

As I thought of different parts of my ex-husband to char, I noticed a hitchhiker along the side of the road. He held up a sign that read: "Anywhere." It got me to stop. After all, it was where I was headed.

"Thanks for pulling over." His Australian accent was music to my ears. I hadn't heard one for a while. Flashes of a trip to Sydney came back to me.

"Sure. Hop in. We're going to the same place."

He opened the passenger door and slid into the leather seat. He threw a duffel bag onto the back seat with his sign. "Any place where you're going, darling, is good for me."

He buckled in as I pulled from the curb. I looked to my right as I checked my mirror. Not bad. I hadn't met an Australian man that looked ugly. His blond hair was warmed by the sun. His blue eyes met mine with a smile as he said, "So thanks for stopping. Not many people helping me out around here. What made you stop?"

"Your sign is where I've decided to go right now." I looked him over. He was all kinds of yummy. Definitely worth stopping for.

"Glad we're going the same direction then." He looked me over with a smile.

I pulled the car back into traffic as he grabbed the seatbelt over his shoulder. Looking in my rearview mirror, I tried to start some conversation. Driving to anywhere was going to take awhile. "So tell me, what brings you up here? You sound like you're from Australia."

He fastened the buckle together with a click. "Melbourne originally. Lived in Sydney a while until I had a craving to see the world." He leaned back in his seat. "Thought I'd do it the ol'-fashioned way," he said holding up his thumb.

"You know it's dangerous to hitchhike?" I said in a teasing voice.

"You know it's dangerous to pick up hitchhikers?" He fired back at me, smirking. "But really, you don't look like you're going to take me into the back woods somewhere and kill me."

"How do you know? I might be a lot more dangerous than I look. Woman in Jaguars are notoriously wicked." I smiled as I looked him up and down.

His dimple winked at me as he laughed. "I've always liked a woman with spirit. You know, they have a good radio station out here. Mostly classic rock, but it usually has a beat."

He reached up to the dash and turned on the radio. AC/DC blasted from the stereo with the chorus to "Hell's Bells." It was just what the doctor ordered. There was the comfortable silence that was ushered in by good rock music. With the music blasting, the windows open, and the good-looking Australian sitting next to me, I was beginning to feel things were looking up. I might even let him live after all this. The ringing of my phone interrupted the music, and I let it ring.

"Are you going to get it?" asked the Aussie.

"Not wanting to. It's probably him."

"Is he the sort of fella that will keep calling?"

"Yes." I knew I was going to have to talk to the bastard eventually. Putting it off wasn't going to help any. I hit the phone button on the steering wheel, and Rich's voice came through the speakers.

"Catherine? Babe? You there?"

"Yes." I was feeling sulky. I wasn't going to let Rich talk me into going back. I had Aussie insurance now. My new boy toy would be a good distraction. I looked over at the Aussie. He did have a wicked-looking torso.

Rich interrupted with another annoying plea. "Cat, really, come back. I'll make it up to you."

"Nothing is going to keep your dick in your pants, Rich. You're free to fuck who you want now. Our marriage is over. I'm not renewing our vows. Goodbye." I hit the disconnect button. It made me feel stronger to just finally shut Rich up. Motioning to the Aussie, I pointed to my purse. "You could do me a big favor and shut off my iPhone?"

"Will do." He scrambled through my bag, pulled out my iPhone, and hit the off button. He admired the rhinestone casing with the Hello Kitty design. He didn't say anything after that. Wise choice. I didn't feel like explaining it. Not yet at least.

"How about you turn the radio back on?" I added in a change-the-subject tone.

He reached out and hit the radio button. Fleetwood Mac soothed my nerves as we continued. I thought this would be a good time to talk about anything else but what happened. "So what's your name?"

"Jeff."

"Jeff what?"

"Jeff Phillips. Yours?"

"Catherine Banks. I usually go by Cat or Cathy."

"Nice meeting you. Have any plans other than going anywhere?"

"Not really. Got any suggestions?"

"Sure. I've always wanted to go to Vegas."

"Vegas sounds like a good change. I think we can cross over the mountains to Hwy 5 and get there through Tahoe." I turned up the music. Suddenly, Vegas sounded like exactly what I needed.

# Chapter 4

Where Hwy 1 met Hwy 101, we headed south. A change in direction was good, and having a destination was helping my mood. A gorgeous, blond Aussie sitting next to me was helping it even more.

He didn't say much, and when we stopped for gas, he left for the restroom. I headed into the store and picked up some drinks and snacks. I didn't know what Jeff would like, so I got a variety, knowing something would surely appeal. I never knew a man that didn't eat something offered from a pretty woman.

When he got back, I had the Jag loaded up and ready to go. "Vegas, here we come."

I had my sunglasses on and thought my THELMA AND LOUISE imitation was looking pretty good right now. I checked my lipstick in the mirror as he put on his seatbelt.

"Looks like we're putting in for some distance. You planning on driving all night?"

"No, figured I'd stop in Clearlake. This lady has got to have a bath." He gave me a long, knowing look. "I don't mind sharing a room." He still had a smile on his face, but said nothing. "I promised a ride to Vegas. I meant it. I just don't want to push all night. And I do need a bath."

"That's kind of why I'm smiling. It's the bath I'm imagining."

I gave him a look. His flirting was going to keep him alive much longer. "Really, I need a bath." I pulled out onto the road.

"It would help if you describe it more clearly. What were you thinking?"

I thought I'd play along, but kept my eyes on the road for now. "Lots of bubbles."

"Go on."

"Lather, and my hair up. I'll have candles lighting the whole room."

"What scent?"

"Rose vanilla. But sometimes," I paused. He was hanging on my every word. I was letting him. Sort of like letting the spider play with the fly. I wasn't sure that he was something I needed yet. But it was good to have the insurance along with me. "It's fun to have a bubble fight, especially if I have someone to play with." I moved my hand down to open up my blouse a little more. I caught his eyes looking as I took a big breath making my chest heave.

I decided that we could explore this direction later tonight. But I wanted to make some miles before the sun got all the way down. Rich would be more powerful then, and I wanted to shield down in a hotel before he started a search sweep for me. I changed the subject.

"Know any good stations around here?"

"Besides the classic rock stations?" He paused to think, catching onto the change of subject. There was a sense of disappointment. Good. At least there was some interest to work with later. "There is a good jazz and blues station. Sometimes plays folk music. So you have to catch it at the right time."

"Let me see if I can find it." I pushed the button and swept through the channels. We got through a Christian rock station, pop, and then hit the jazz station. "There, that's better."

The music helped the distance pass by as I turned from 101 to Hwy 20. It would be a beautiful drive until we hit Hwy 5. The turns would help ease my sense of dread of the confrontation with Rich. I was going to have to beat him, or kill him. Neither outcome was going to be pretty.

A couple of times, Jeff's eyes drifted to look me over. I let my mind focus on the road. Redwoods soared above, creating a shady canopy. I opened the windows to let in some of the fresh air. It's the one thing I loved about California. There are so many things close by. You could be driving the coast and then drive up into the coastal mountains, all within thirty minutes. Some parts of Hwy 1 were unique experiences, with redwoods to ocean cliffs back to forests. The extremes of Northern California mixed well with my mood. If I didn't watch it, I'd be driving down toward Calistoga for a mud bath and wine tasting. But Vegas was calling. A new state had new opportunities.

I noticed it was also getting dark. We were near Upper Lake. Breaking the driving silence, I motioned to Jeff. "You think you could work the map in my iPhone and find a place to stay for the night."

"Sure." He seemed to be off in his own thoughts. "It's in your purse still right?"

"Yeah. Go ahead and grab it out of the pocket on the inside. It's the zippered one. By the way," I turned to catch his eye. "It's nice that you asked."

"I know a woman's purse is her most prized possession. It's always good to ask first before rummaging through it." He winked as he grabbed my phone. God, he was gorgeous. I scanned his biceps through my peripheral vision. His jeans fit tight in the right places, while his T-shirt hugged his chest. I noted the curve of his chest. I was getting the inkling to explore him soon.

He started looking around. "Where are we?"

"I saw a sign that mentioned Upper Lake."

"Right."

He launched the map app, and I kept driving. "Okay, if we follow the road for five more miles, we'll come to a turn off for the next town. Take that turn, and it looks like there is a hotel on the right. It's called the Twin Burrows Inn."

"Got it." We'd lost the jazz station in the woods, and I had tried some other stations along the way to no avail. After a while, I couldn't drive with static, so I'd left it off for the last hour. All I heard was wind and road noise as we made a turn down a deserted main street. The place was dead quiet. Nothing much out here in the country; even the Denny's looked closed.

"Turn here."

I saw a sign for Twin Burrows Inn and made a right. I parked the Jag and got out. "You going to come in, or should I just check us in?"

"After you." Jeff opened the door and motioned to the hotel. "We can always come back for the baggage."

"I don't have much, except for the mental kind."

He smiled as I got out. "That's more than what I got, love. I mostly carry my sleeping bag and a change of clothes in my duffel. A man doesn't need much more." He shut the door and started walking toward the lobby.

"Toothbrush?"

"Okay, maybe one of those." The gravel crunched under his feet as we crossed to the walkway up to the main office. He opened the door for me, and I smiled. I noted his bemused look as I walked to the counter. Again, he was definitely adding points to living longer in my book. I kept looking at how his jeans hugged his ass, and his T-shirt didn't make it hard to imagine the defined muscles underneath. My favorite part of any man was his chest. I was trying not to drool as I walked into the lobby.

"One room please."

The man at the desk looked up. He looked over to both of us. His face blossomed with a plastic smile. He'd probably seen so many couples. We couldn't faze him. "Double or single beds?"

"Two beds please," I answered without missing a beat.

The man retrieved the needed paperwork, and I filled it out. "King or queen?"

I looked at Jeff, and he answered, "Whatever you got."

"I'll check for rooms available." The man typed in our information and looked up again. "We've got a double with queen beds. Paying by credit card?"

I dug through my purse and handed him my credit card.

He continued the usual questions in a robotic manner. "Will you be staying more than one night?"

"Just one."

"One or two keys."

I turned to Jeff. "You want your own key?"

"You're my ride. Where you go, I go."

I turned back to the man. "One key, then."

"Fine." He went back to running my credit card, and then turned the paper for me to sign. "Fill in here and here." He pointed to the hotel agreement, and I signed and initialled. It always seems like you are signing your life away whenever you get a room.

"Okay, you're checked in for one night. Check out time is eleven a.m., and the bar and restaurant will be open for about two more hours. Enjoy your stay."

I turned to Jeff. "I think it's time I bought you a drink. It's good to have someone along for the ride."

"I thought the man was supposed to buy the drinks."

"Don't worry. You can pay me back in some other ways later." I gave him a wink as we went into the bar.

They didn't have the good port like at the last bar. I had to settle for a white zinfandel. But the wine had the same effect. Poor Jeff had to settle for American beer instead of a lager. But at least it was some local brew that seemed to satisfy him.

"So, if you don't mind me asking," I began. "Are you finding yourself in the States, or just traveling?"

"A little of both," he replied between sips. "I thought I'd get out and see things before I settled down to some respectful career. I graduated in February."

I took a sip as I studied his collarbone. I wanted to start tracing my finger down all over the front of his chest. I wanted to nuzzle next to his neck. One more glass of wine, and I was going to start putting my thoughts into action. "What did you get your degree in?"

"Economics and computer design."

"Hmm." I felt like purring. "Beautiful and brainy."

"I was going to say that about you."

Unfortunately, the waiter placed down our food orders, interrupting my thought about diving for his lips. He was looking more luscious by the minute. I needed some food to fill my empty stomach. But I was thinking something else needed to be filled to relieve my aching soul.

"So what did you want to see in the States?" I said after swallowing a bite of my club sandwich. I followed it down with more wine as he answered.

"Michigan. And of course, Vegas."

"Why Michigan?"

"I've got a sister I want to visit."

Damn, he had family in the States. It might be obvious if I accidentally killed him or Rich. This could get ugly fast. I was growing rather attached to him, and didn't want him to get in the way.

"Well, at least we can get the one place off your bucket list. Michigan might be a bit of a stretch right now for me. I've got baggage I'd love to unload on you, but really, you're here to enjoy yourself."

"I'm guessing the man on the phone is your baggage."

"Kinda like that." I took another bite of my sandwich. "He's a real prime example of who not to trust."

"And you'd trust a hitchhiker you found on the highway?" He smiled and took a bite of his hamburger. Juice dribbled down his chin, and I tried not to imagine licking it off. He got it with the back of his hand.

"Yes. A hitchhiker is more trustworthy than an asshole that slept with my best friend."

Jeff shook his head at that. "That is really low, even for most men. I'm sorry to hear that Catherine. You deserve better."

It was nice to hear it from someone else. I could say it a thousand times, but someone else saying it made it stick better. "Tell me about it."

He laughed. "I've been there, darling."

I looked up. He had my rapt attention. "Was it your best friend?"

"No, my brother. He slept with my girlfriend. Still haven't quite forgiven him, since he married her after."

"Shit. That does suck."

He nodded as he took another bite of his burger. "I figure love makes you do weird things. It's the attraction that gets you. Sometimes you can't fight it."

I nodded. "Yeah, I know what you mean." I took another sip of wine. This was becoming a harder situation. I didn't want him to die, but could I let him live? There was only one way to find out. I downed the last of my wine. "Come on. I have an idea."

He jammed a fry in his mouth and sat up. "All right. Any clues to what that might be?"

"I'll have to show you."

# Chapter 5

Throwing money on the table, I grabbed his hand and pulled him from the booth. I led him to the elevator.

"What did you have in mind?" He hit the button and leaned toward me.

"You'll have to wait and see." I leaned into his neck and whispered into his ear. "Keeps you guessing."

"Do I get three guesses?" he whispered back.

"Yes, but you only have until the elevator arrives," I said, looking at the elevator count down the floors as it came down to pick us up.

"Is it bigger than a bread basket?"

"Yes." I grinned, moving away to see if my bait was working, and looked back at the numbers. Four, three... Why was it taking so long? I hit the button to get it to move faster.

"Is it smaller than a thimble?"

"That depends on what you do with it." I smiled at him, as he leaned closer to me again. I could feel his breath near the back of my neck as I still watched the elevator's progress.

"Is it something that needs a lot of rubbing?" He started to wrap his arms around my waist, grabbing me from behind.

"You can think of yourself as Aladdin. I'm the lamp."

I heard the ping of the elevator arriving, and pulled him into the elevator. The door closed, and I leaned into him, practically falling on him as he grabbed me again. He pulled me closer, and we connected in the right places. I could feel the warmth of his back, the scent of his hair, and he started to explore my hips and down my thighs.

I turned, and he met my lips, diving in for the need for each other, burning for the connection finally made. Our kiss was explosive. He knew the right amount of suction on my lower lip to bring shivers up my leg. I wrapped my arms around his neck. I stopped thinking about anything else but getting closer and feeling my breasts rub against his chest. The warmth between my legs grew as the elevator doors opened.

I led the way with the key, looking at the room numbers to match the doors. "Two-thirteen, here it is." I slid the key card in, waiting for the light to change from red to green. There was the satisfying click of entry, and I pushed the door open. I threw my purse to the floor as he grabbed my waist again, and pulled me into another kiss.

I came up for air and pointed at the door. "Shouldn't we probably close that?"

"Maybe." Jeff kicked it with his foot, and picked me up to carry me to one of the beds.

Damn. His biceps had been teasing me all day. I relished the feel of grabbing onto his arms as he lowered me carefully to the bedspread. He followed me down as we formed one intertwined mass.

I reached for his T-shirt and pulled it over his head. Finally. I started caressing down his deeply tanned skin, tracing the definition down to his waist. I closed my eyes to feel the sensation of his bare skin beneath my fingers. I felt the texture of his chest hair as it led me to lower territory.

I could smell the odor of his spicy skin radiating a heat that intoxicated me. Washing over me like wine, I started to crawl over the top of him. I let my tongue flutter rapidly over his exposed chest taking in the sharp, tang of his skin. His spice over powered me as I swept my tongue around his nipples. He let out a groan as he cradled my head.

I started feeling his lower abdomen below me, flickering my tongue fast down between his pectorals, and down to his waist. His sculptured stomach glided below my hands as I headed for the bulge between his legs. I explored his jeans, looking for the zipper that would free him. I pulled the zipper while reaching around the back to feel his tight buns. Then, I pulled the jeans down, looking at him. He was arching his back slightly, and looking like Adonis.

I gave the jeans a final tug and crawled over him, grabbing around the waistband of his briefs. "Ready?"

"As ever," he answered.

I tugged down, letting his member fall free. I threw the briefs behind me and grabbed his shaft. Licking the tip first, I spread my lips around his cock and moved down. Taking him in as far as I could, I began the rapid movement up and down that would bring him to a climax. I loved the feeling of control I had when I could bring a man to pleasure. I felt I had him where I wanted him.

I felt him grow harder within my mouth. Bringing him close to the edge, I pulled my mouth away to let my hands stroke him into a frenzy. But I didn't want him to loose his climax yet. I wanted to have my turn.

"Tag. You're it now," I said as I threw myself next to him.

He grabbed and trapped me below him. Just where I wanted to be. He unbuttoned each individual blouse button, slowly, drawing his finger down. My skin shivered with anticipation. He slipped the blouse over my shoulders exposing me in my silver lace bra. Laughing, I sprung my girls free, as he caught the bra and flung it to hang on a lampshade.

He took me all in with one stare. "Damn, you are one fine woman."

"Want to see the rest?" I sat up in my cotton shorts and undid the front button.

"Let me." He said unzipping my shorts. He pulled them down and started on my undies. He pushed me back, holding me as he nuzzled the side of my neck. Then, one by one, he started small kisses down the sides of my body until he reached my stomach. My insides were melting as he moved his lips over me, licking my stomach and grabbing my underwear in his teeth.

A sensation shot up my sides as he pulled my undies lower and lower. I could feel his breath as he glided my panties down my legs. Each puff hit my thighs, and between my legs. Tingles shot through my body as I arched my back. He made his way slowly down my body.

Fits of longing hit me as he pulled my underwear lower. I wanted this man inside me. Finally, he removed my lace undies over my toes.

Crawling back over me, he kissed the sides of my stomach, my breasts, and the side of my neck. Shivers went up to my head and down my middle to my groin. I felt like I was being played like a violin. Jeff was definitely hitting some chords. The heat was building between us, and an explosion was heading my direction. My wetness between my legs was throbbing for attention.

I felt his full weight of his chest press against my bare breasts. I wrapped my arms around him and flipped us over so I was on top.

"Sometimes I like to drive."

His smile grew bigger. Slowly, I sat up and guided his member into me. I came down again and again until I had him firmly inside. Then, I began rocking back and forth, moving over my pleasure spot, building and building, until I was ready for release. I felt the moment pass through me, as I shuttered to perfection.

I collapsed on him, kissing him, and smelling his spicy, masculine scent. I waited a few moments before I whispered, "Do you want a try now?"

"Is it my turn to open the bottle?"

"Open me, please."

He flipped on top of me and started kissing me, deeper this time. Longer and wetter, he started kissing down my chest. Sucking gently on my nibbles, he circled them as he continued down my stomach, flicking his tongue as he progressed down.

He reached between my legs and I opened my thighs, leaning back. He flicked down to my wet opening, circling my clit with his tongue. I could feel the sensations building inside me, as he pulled me closer to climax. He took his finger, rubbing my clit faster and faster. He stroked my passion within me until I couldn't take it much longer.

"Please, " I said grabbing the sheets. "Now."

He ended everything by thrusting into me. I felt him enter. Each thrust of movement built me more and more. I could feel him between my thighs taking over my body and commanding it to respond. Thrust after thrust, we joined together in our passion. The final release came, and he collapsed on me, breathing fast, and I held him until I felt his member loosen, and become free of our union.

"Thank you," I said kissing him as we lay next to each other. "I think I've come to the conclusion of what I needed."

"What was that?" Jeff answered as he cupped my chin for another kiss.

I slowly broke from his embrace to answer, "Freedom."

# Chapter 6

Morning broke with a fresh start. I rolled over to give a kiss to Jeff. He returned it with no hesitation. Always a good sign. I showered and got dressed as he watched me from the bed. "Really, we should get on the road."

"What's your hurry?"

"I have a feeling my ex might be trying to find me."

"And this is worrying you because?" He sat up on his elbow.

Drying my hair with a towel, I answered, "It won't be pretty when he finds me. It might be quite a battle." That was an understatement. It was most likely to be a raging battle of spells that could destroy a whole town. It's another reason why I was trying to head to the desert. If we were going to meet somewhere, it was better not to fry the surrounding area.

"I'm not afraid of him," Jeff said. "I can take anything he'd have to say."

I wrapped my hair in the towel and started getting dressed. "It's not what he'll say, but what he'll do." I put on a tight beige skirt and a burgundy blouse over the lace bra. The sea-glass necklace and matching earrings made me feel like a new me, and I wanted to sparkle.

"You don't need to worry. I can take him, really. I'm not worried if he comes after me." He gave me a kiss I returned eagerly.

I looked into his deep blue eyes and wanted to believe him. All I wanted was to be free of Richard. But now, I didn't want Jeff involved. This was not going to be a pretty situation. He might not survive. "Yes, I just want to be done with Rich, the bastard. But it's dangerous to be with me right now. He'll want revenge for leaving him. He likes to be in control even more than I do."

I winked at him, remembering my chance to drive on top last night. Damn. It was starting to hit me. I was overwhelmed by the memory of Cassandra and Richard in bed together. His loving caress of her arm. Her shocked look as she saw me enter the room. Oh. He deserved more than to be blasted in the pool. I must have swooned a bit as the memory engulfed me. Jeff grabbed me closer and held me. That's when I started to cry.

It felt good to release the feelings that had built up. The shock was wearing off as the reality hit me. Rich really did sleep with my best friend. It helped to have someone there with me to just hold me. Jeff didn't say anything, but let me have my time to compose myself. I finally wiped my eyes and sniffed. "Bastard."

"Feeling better?" He let me go a little.

"I think I just needed a bit of a melt down."

"You've been through a lot."

"It's just that I can't get the image of Cassandra and him together out of my head. It just hurts." I was on the verge of tears again.

"And last night?" he ended the phrase as a question.

I looked up at him. "Was a night I'll never forget. But I'm just," I stopped for a moment a bit dizzy. "Very overwhelmed and confused. A lot has happened in the last forty-eight hours. But I know one thing." I made sure he was looking at me. "You're the best thing that has happened so far." I grabbed his hand.

He hugged me close and held me until I felt ready to face the future. I wiped my eyes and said, "I think we can do this. I just want to make sure you understand that there might be danger involved. I'm getting rather fond of you. I'd hate to see you get some holes in the wrong places." I know what he might assume with that comment. I just didn't mention how big a hole a well-placed fireball could make.

"Don't worry. I can handle myself."

I left him to think of the mortal danger he imagined. It would be hard to explain the real danger.

We packed the few things we had and went down to check out. We dropped off the key card and headed to the Jag. I counted my positives. I was with a really gorgeous Aussie, and it was a beautiful travel day to make some miles. I'd try not to think about what might be ahead. I sank into the leather seat, with Jeff looking at me.

"Think you can get more jazz, or something on the radio?"

"Sure thing." Jeff started playing with the dial as I backed out.

It was a hundred miles down the road that I noticed the black sedan following us. Of course, Hwy 20 goes on for miles. But it should have turned or done something by the time we merged with Hwy 5. I picked up speed and it matched. I tried changing lanes and it didn't pass me. Something was up.

"Have you noticed that we're being followed?"

"What makes you think so," asked Jeff looking over toward me. He'd been busy looking out the window. The towering redwoods had given way to the open expanse of fields and sleepy farming towns in Central California. He'd been staring at them for some time. I think my comment startled him.

"Um, the black sedan. Look in the side mirror."

He looked over by the window, and nodded. "I see it. How long has it been back there?"

"Not sure. There's one way to find out if it's following us. Pull off at the next exit. Do we need gas yet?"

"Wouldn't hurt to get some."

"Then, let's do a pit stop and see if it follows us."

I congratulated myself for picking up Jeff as I turned off at the next exit. Having another opinion was helping to keep my freak-out level under control. I hated confrontation, unless I had to fight. Then, it was SAYONARA. When pushed into a corner, I came out fighting. Jeff was keeping me from feeling like I was in a corner. He seemed to always have a plan.

I pulled into a Chevron station and parked next to a pump. Jeff got out and walked over to the convenience store. I went over to the pump and realized I needed to swipe my card. I went back to the car to get it out of my purse. That's when I saw the black sedan drive into another island. A man got out and started working the pump. I didn't recognize him. He was dressed in khaki shorts and a T-shirt. I looked back to my purse and dug out my card. Jeff returned just as I was finishing filling up the tank.

I ducked my head in the window. "I've got to use the restroom. By the way, the black sedan is right over there. No, don't look that way." I stopped him in mid turn.

He shrugged his shoulders. "Maybe you're just being paranoid. It's been an emotional forty-eight hours, Catherine."

"No, I'm sure it's following us. If we take our time, maybe he'll pull out first. If he's following though, he'll probably wait."

I grabbed my purse and headed for the ladies' room. I went to the cashier and got the key. Heading out the door to the side of the store, I saw the black sedan pull away. Relief overwhelmed me. Wow. I must have been feeling really insecure. After restroom usage, I returned to the Jag.

"I saw it leave," I said to Jeff as I got in.

"Yeah. Chalk it up to your unsettled feelings. Most likely, they're making you spook at anything."

"Probably. But you don't know my ex. He's the kind that would hire someone to find and follow me."

I drove for another hour and started to feel a rumble. My stomach rolled like thunder. I looked at the car's digital clock. It was almost one o'clock. "I guess it's lunch time." My words were accented by another stomach gurgle.

"I should say so." Jeff grinned. "Really, I was starting to feel hungry too."

The next exit had a road sign for food, so I pulled off.

Every truck stop café has got to have a cookie cutter designer. They all look the same. They've all got tan, vinyl booths and a coffee counter. A country twang was playing in the background. The floor had the sticky residue of mountains of grease from years of serving gut-busting cholesterol bombs.

"Take any booth you like. I'll be right over." A waitress with her hair up, apron, and a pencil behind her ear was serving some older regulars at the coffee counter. It was like walking into any dive coffee shop in the US. If everyone was staring at me, with my burgundy silk blouse, sunglasses, and impeccable lipstick, it wasn't because I wasn't trying. I did scream city girl when I walked in the door. This was definitely not my territory. There was only one-way to progress, looking fabulous.

I smoothed my skirt and walked over, confident in my newfound freedom. I slid into the booth, perched my sunglasses on my head, and looked around. Jeff slid in across from me. He'd taken his time. I guess he wasn't into making an entrance.

I looked around as some of the regulars from the coffee counter stared back. "A bit of a dive, you think?"

"No, it's got a realistic charm. Notice this." Jeff grabbed the menus from the holder and pointed to a stain. "Real ketchup."

"You could taste it. You are an expert at licking."

"So what you both want?" The waitress towered over us, pulling a pencil from behind her ear. My comment didn't even seem to faze her.

"Club sandwich and iced tea for me," I answered.

She looked at Jeff.

"I think I'll have the cheeseburger," he answered.

"Bacon on that?"

"Yes. And a Coke. And if you've got barbeque sauce, could you add it to the burger?"

"Sure will, honey. We're known for our ribs. I bet you'd love them. We have free samples. Would you like a sample plate? Most the regulars are hooked once they try them."

"I do," I piped up. "I don't usually eat pig, but I feel like doing naughty things from now on."

"Some oink samples coming right up. Be back with your drinks in a sec." She winked as she left and put the order up on a metal carousel for the cook.

"You know, I think Vegas is going to be great." I grabbed his hands. It was good to have contact. I could feel his returned squeeze.

"I have no doubt," he answered, smiling. He kept that long stare, like he kept eating me up. I know I was delicious to look at. I had the spells to back that up. But he seemed to enjoy extra long stare downs.

"I could use some on-the-edge action. Like rolling the dice, and seeing what happens."

"Figuratively or for real?"

"Both. I've never shot craps. I want to try new things from now on. No limits."

Our moment of big rollers was interrupted as the waitress placed down our drinks. I started doctoring my ice tea. Just one pack of sugar would be enough. I carefully stirred with my straw. "You know, freedom is a newer concept for me. Just doing what I want and when. It's been a long time since I've done that."

"I've got my whole trip planned out to basically follow on the whim." Jeff sipped his soda. "No maps, no cars or trains unless I feel like it. Whatever hits my fancy. I'm blowing with the wind."

"Like Forrest Gump?"

"Kind of, but no shrimp involved. Allergic."

"Oh, sorry." I shrugged. "That must be hard to deal with."

"Not really. Most restaurants are pretty good if you tell them up front."

"But burgers are no problem."

"Absolutely." He smiled and went back to his soda.

God, he looked gorgeous. I was hungry for more than food right now. But my stomach gave a grumble. Well, maybe there were different kinds of hunger. One thing at a time.

I continued figuring out where to head next. "After Hwy 5, we probably could cut through to Tahoe or go all the way down to LA. Your choice, I'm enjoying the drive."

"I haven't been to Tahoe yet. I came in through LA. So I got a good look around before heading north. Mostly I thumbed the coast. What's in Tahoe?"

"A really big lake. Can't miss it. In fact, it's got incredible skiing during the winter. This time of year, snow has melted, and a lot of the summer crowds are gone since school started. September is a great time to go."

"Sounds like it's doable."

I was starting to enjoy getting to know Jeff a bit better. But the food arrived, and I felt this overwhelming urge to attack my sandwich. I was ravenous. It had been a long couple of days. For the first time, I think I was starting to relax.

Then, I glanced out the window. The black sedan we'd noticed before pulled up to the diner. Shit. I knew things were going too well.

# Chapter 7

Jeff stopped eating and turned his head to follow my gaze.

He put his burger down. "It might not be the same car."

The same guy with khaki shorts and a T-shirt got out and walked to the door. "What should we do?" I had put down my sandwich and looked to Jeff for a next move.

"He's probably just heading our direction." He grabbed his burger and took another bite.

"I hope so." But I lowered my sunglasses over my eyes and started sipping the iced tea. If I hid parts of my face, it couldn't hurt.

The guy walked to the counter, and the waitress did her normal routine of choose your own booth. He walked past me and kept going.

"Is he sitting yet?"

Jeff finished a bite. "He's sitting at the back counter and has a menu out. He's probably just hungry like the rest of us. Come on, it's a long way to Vegas. We need to eat."

I got back to chowing down, but had lost my momentum. I wanted to turn around and see the guy behind me. There was something familiar in the way that he moved his body. That nonchalant arrogance reminded me of Richard. Then I knew. Oh shit. It couldn't be.

The stranger motioned to the waitress. "A coffee, please."

The one thing Richard forgot to disguise was his voice. The waitress walked over to the counter and asked for his order as I said, "That's him."

"Who?"

I leaned forward. "Richard. He's got a disguise on. But I know his voice. It's him."

Jeff took another bite of his burger. He swallowed and took a sip of his drink. "You sure it's him?"

"Absolutely. We've got to get out of here." I didn't want things to go bad fast.

But they did.

The stranger looked over at me and smiled. This time, he saluted me with his coffee. That wasn't good. Then, he started walking over.

"Come on," I motioned to Jeff. "I think we need to get out of here fast."

"I'm not scared of what he has to say."

"It's not what he'll say, remember?"

Just as he got close, Richard let his cloaking spell drop. There he was, all six foot two inches of him, staring down at me with a big, silly grin. "Want to reconcile?"

"Really, Richard. I thought you had more originality than this. How did you find me?"

"Tracking device on the bottom of your car. Never can be too careful. Don't have to rely on magic when you've got technology."

Shit. I forgot how much he loved his gadgets. I should have known better.

He stared Jeff up and down. "I see you've been busy."

"Not as much as you. Cassandra and you will make a lovely couple."

"Really, think I'd settle for a mortal after you?"

Oh. I wasn't going to fall for flattery. Stand strong, girl. I kept a mental picture of blasting him against the wall. I started building a shield around Jeff and me. To my surprise, I felt a surge gather and guide my energy between us. It wasn't Richard. He kept smiling at the two of us.

"Hello, Jeff." Rich nodded to Jeff and his smiled broadened.

Jeff nodded back. "Richard."

Okay, now I had to look at them both. "You two know each other?"

Richard eyed me a bit shockingly. "Most warlocks are familiar with each other. But Jeff and I go way back."

I looked back at Jeff. I felt him grab the energy I was building and lock down a strong shield around us. I held onto some of my energy, holding it ready just in case. I now had two warlocks in front of me. "Wait. I'm running away from one warlock and run right into the arms of another?"

Richard laughed in answer. "Sure did, honey. Not only that, one of my best friends for several decades. I'd say we're even now."

"Shit." I really did feel the redness of my face. I'm sure I was several shades of red. I would have blasted them both right then. But two against one is bad odds.

As soon as Richard saw my face, he cracked up. "You didn't know, did you?" His laughter just made me more pissed off.

"If you don't want a fireball up your ass, I'd advise leaving now."

"I have to warn you, Jeff, when she's mad, give her room." Richard smiled as he barrelled on, "You know, I was going to see if you wanted to give it another go. But I see you've definitely moved on." He winked at Jeff. "Take care of her. I wish you a lot of luck. You're going to need it."

Richard went over to the counter, threw down a bill, and walked out the door of the coffee shop.

I slowly looked at Jeff. Lucky for him, he had a guilty look on his face. "Why didn't you tell me?"

"I'm sorry, Cat. I could tell you were a witch, but you were so upset. I thought it was Rich when I heard him on the phone. But I wasn't sure until just now. I'm surprised too."

"Yeah. Sucks that you know him. But it's worse that you didn't tell me you're a warlock."

"You didn't ask."

I held back my tears. "That doesn't mean you shouldn't tell me."

Jeff tried to hold my hand, but I didn't return the pressure. He continued with a diatribe of excuses. "I've been traveling among mortals for a while. I haven't met up with a witch for a while. It has been some time since I've been in the States. In fact, it was during a fierce battle that I last saw Rich. We were on the same side if that helps any."

I was still fighting the floodgates. I was so near the edge. "I feel so betrayed. I wouldn't have done anything had I known you were Rich's friend. I wasn't trying to get revenge. I'm just trying to sort myself out."

"No, don't cry, Cat." He gripped my hand more to get me to focus. "I really have wanted to be with you the last few days. Maybe there is a reason we met when we did. It almost seems like fate."

A sniff came out before I could stop it. "All right. I believe you." Another sniff made it dab time. I let go of his hands to dab a napkin at the corner of my eye. "And somehow, I think we've avoided a pretty nasty spell battle." I had to look at the positive. There wasn't going to be any toasted Jeff.

"Well, if I know Rich, he'll find some way to stab back. It will just be when we least expect it. I wouldn't let my guard down yet."

"Right." I noted the fact that he'd said "we" and took a deep breath. I had to put my big girl panties on for this. Besides, I was free of Richard. This was an official move-on moment. I looked across the table at Jeff, with his blue eyes, blond hair, and incredible body. Could I fall in love with a warlock again?

I grabbed his hands, still clinging to the napkin holding my tears. "I'll take a chance if you will?"

He returned the pressure. "Anything is possible if you take a chance."

I smiled. "Sounds like we're ready for Vegas."

We headed out the door of the diner, ready for whatever might come. It was time to take that chance. He turned out to be another warlock, but somehow I felt lucky.

# Never Fall for a Warlock

Beware of Warlocks, Book 2

# Chapter 1

"Hit me." I looked the blackjack dealer square in the eye. He turned over an ace. Blackjack. "Yes." I smiled knowing the cameras in the casino were watching me. It wouldn't be much longer until the House witch spotted me. I never got to play long even without using spells. The House just didn't trust witches. Maybe just one more hand? I felt like pushing my luck. I took a sip of my piña colada. The dealer dealt the next card, and I fingered the table for another hit. Bust.

The dealer placed down an ace. I knew a luck spell would draw too much attention. But I looked around just in case my energies were putting the House witch on alert. I felt the aura of a woman standing by a pillar at the edge of the blackjack tables. Damn, she was a strong one.

She gave me a knowing smile. I lifted a finger and cast a quick draw spell. I felt the lock down of her counter spell around my hand. Shit. The dealer put another card down. The six of spades. I was going to have to finish this hand the old-fashioned way.

I brushed my hand against the table, feeling the counter spell holding my energies in check. Damn it. I hated the pressure around me, keeping me trapped against using magic. The dealer placed another card. Jack of clubs. I let out a sigh as I felt a hand go around my waist.

"Had enough action?" he said over the bing of the slot machines.

I picked up my chips, throwing one at the dealer. "If you've got a room, I'd rather get out of here. I can't play without some counter spell being thrown at me. There are tons of protection layers." I eyed the House witch. I could still feel the shield around my energies. I didn't fight it. I knew they'd just throw me out.

"A witch can't stay in here long," I said as I grabbed my drink.

Jeff laughed at me. "You should know better, Cat. The casinos won't let anyone have an edge, including witches." I tried to keep my pout under control as he held up the key card. "Got us all set. Now if only we can find the elevators."

"I'll hang on to you. It's a frickin' maze in here."

We headed off down one of the carpeted aisles. I stopped and straightened my heels as I got the speed up to slink through the slot machines. Not an easy thing to do when you're balancing your drink.

Jeff looked up at the sign with the arrows pointing in all directions. "Looks like the room elevators are to the right."

"Gotcha." I knocked back the rest of the drink and left the glass on a slot machine. "Lead on. I could use some pool time. Which reminds me, you'll love the new suit I got."

"Can't wait to see you in it." Jeff gave me a knowing look as we crossed the aisle to the corridor that led out of the casino.

We waited for the elevator as I stared at the red carpeting and chandeliers in the lobby, trying to keep my mind off of the shields. It was good to be back in the town that never slept. Vegas tolerated witches more than other cities. In fact, they had some pretty happening underground hot spots just for the witch and undead. I smiled as I remembered some of them.

I shifted on my new heels again as a couple stumbled into us. They pushed the button together.

"Sorry. Seem to be having a bit of trouble getting back to our room." They both burst out laughing. Jeff shrugged. Mortals. It always took three times the alcohol to get a witch buzzed. We have a high tolerance. What would get a witch buzzed would kill a mortal. Sometimes I just felt sorry for them.

"No worries," said Jeff.

"No, I'm sorry," said the man. "We're just trying to figure out if we're even in the right hotel."

I laughed. "It's Vegas. People get messed up. It happens."

"Yeah." The woman gave a bit of a hiccup to her answer. "Shit, yeah."

I heard the slide of the elevator doors and slipped in. The guy sloshed his girlfriend in, and the two of us followed. Jeff asked, "Which floor?"

"Fourteen... I hope."

Jeff pushed fourteen and ten.

They started giggling again as I asked, "Any of this look familiar?"

"Maybe," the guy answered. "I honestly don't remember. Just too fucked up."

The elevator stopped at the tenth floor and the door slid open. "Well, good luck with that. Hope you're in the right place."

"We'll find out soon enough," the woman answered as Jeff and I stepped out and the elevator doors closed behind us.

Jeff turned to me as he glided down the hall. "Should we tell them they aren't in the right hotel?"

"How could you tell," I asked.

"He was waving his keycard around. It wasn't for this hotel. The name looked vaguely familiar. I think they're supposed to be next door."

"Nope." I had an evil glint in my eye. "They'll figure it out, or have fun trying to get in the room upstairs."

"Only in Vegas." He laughed as he slid the key card into our room's lock.

It was your basic suite: mini kitchen, sitting room, and bedroom. You could pretty much move in. Of course, some people did, like Howard Hughes. I guess there is always the option to buy the casino. Then, you'd never have to leave. I like lots of options.

Jeff let out a big yawn. "I think I'll take a quick nap. It was a long drive, and I didn't get much sleep after you took over." He stretched and yawned again as I walked over to my bag to get changed into my bikini and cover up. It was still early in the day, and I was in the mood for some pool time.

I picked up the white strings. "Whatever. I didn't think you would ever get tired. I thought warlocks had tons of energy," I said with a sly grin. "You and Rich do have THAT in common."

"You're not comparing me to your ex-husband again, are you?"

"Not intentionally, but since I found out you were best buds, it's a thought that often crosses my mind."

"As long as you don't hold it against me." He started taking off his shirt. I admired the honed abs and chest as he added, "Most warlocks can sense each other. I'd have known he was there even if he hadn't worn a disguise spell. You had me off my game back in the diner. I would have recognized Rich, but you have that power of distraction even without spells."

"Still, I wish you'd told me," I said as I pulled off one of my earrings and headed to the bathroom to change.

"About being a warlock, or about being friends with your ex?" he said with a crooked smile.

I should have known that Jeff was a warlock, too, not just a lone Aussie hitchhiker that I picked up on Hwy 1. It seems I can't help but be attracted to warlocks. They just get in my blood, like an addiction. Not to mention I have the worst luck with warlocks. Give me a good mortal, and I can play with him like a cat with a mouse. But, I was still deciding whether he was the warlock for me. Warlocks could be dangerous. Maybe I just needed some air, or fewer warlocks.

I got into my fabulous bikini, cover-up, white brimmed hat, and leather sandals. Then, I grabbed a towel. When I opened the door, I turned and watched him lying on the bed, still in his jeans, zonked out. Okay. Maybe he really was tired. How can you believe what a man is really thinking? Wish I had a spell for that.

I made sure I had my room card in my cover-up pocket and headed for the door. Snoring was pouring steadily from the bed. I took one last look. Lying there with his eyes closed, Jeff looked like a sleeping marble god. The diffused daylight through the curtains cast a soft white glow on his skin. He was gorgeous, and was of no use to me. I felt frustrated like a cat in heat.

Maybe I just needed some eye candy by the pool instead. Some new scenery might help me deal with my man woes. Not only did I need to get over what my husband had done. I had to ask myself which hurt more — my husband's betrayal or the fact that the new guy who I was trying to get over it with was also Rich's best friend. I sighed. Nothing to do but get some air and pool time. I always thought better frying in the sun.

I headed for the elevator. Maybe I needed another drink. Or two. Or three. I had to account for my higher tolerance for alcohol. No worries. Vegas always had plenty on hand. But drinking wasn't going to help me forget the image of Cassandra in bed with Rich. A best friend just doesn't do her friend's husband. I should have blasted her with the force spell. Just throwing him into our pool wasn't satisfying enough. I needed something equally satisfying to get rid of this frustration. I pushed the button to the pool, and waited.

The elevator made several stops on the way down. Each time, more people crammed inside. Within minutes, the pool floor finally arrived. I got out and walked around looking for the right lounge chair. The palm trees waved in the breeze above the various people lying around the wade pool. Most looked single from their body language and auras. I wasn't sure whether I fit in the singles' scene or the just-not-interested crowd.

I found the chair closest to the wade pool and staked out a claim. Arranging the towel, I got into true sun-worship position. Now, I just needed a waiter. I checked for any shielding spells. Nope, nothing here but one blockage spell to ward off luck. I flipped my hand and flashed an urgent need spell through the air. I had a waiter asking for my drink within seconds.

"What would be your pleasure?"

"Piña colada, stat."

I lowered my sunglasses and closed my eyes. I could feel the sun warming my skin, baking away everything that had happened. My white bikini highlighted my tan in the right places. My white brimmed hat shielded my eyes from most of the glare, so I could sit back and relax. Pool time was reflective time. I was going to miss my pool back in California. Rich would probably get the house. He's the one that wanted it by the beach anyway. But I was going to miss the pool.

Then there was my Aussie rebound, Jeff. Jeff was a lot of fun, but he had turned into Mr. Complication overnight. The fact that he knew Rich, and worse, was his best friend and a warlock, too, had created a lot of complications. Don't get me wrong, the rebound-sex was amazing. But maybe I needed another new start. I'd broken my new number-one rule, never fall for a warlock again. Granted, I didn't know he was a warlock when the fall began.

I felt the sun blocked, and said, "Just put it on the table, please."

"I would if it would fit," said an unfamiliar voice in front of me.

I sat up and opened my eyes. Damn, if this wasn't a sight to behold. A superb hunk of hot, bulging, muscled flesh straight out of a Vegas strip show was standing before me covered with a crisp dress shirt hugging a well-formed chest. He had a gorgeous, chiselled face, a Pierce Brosnan look with piercing blue eyes stared back at me. "You're not the waiter," I said, a little dumbfounded.

"Do you want me to be?"

"Depends on what you serve."

"Careful, honey. You might get what you ask for." His Irish accent sent shivers between my legs. There is nothing sexier than a foreign accent.

He smiled as he slid onto the lounge chair beside me with the ease and grace of a practiced dancer. This time, I tried a spell check. No shielding, and he appeared human.

"Liam O'Neil." He pointed to the deck chair beside me. "May I?"

"Catherine. A man with manners. I like that. Some might consider you old fashioned." He was catching my attention. I noticed he had a cute butt before sitting on it. That was a step in the right direction.

"Not at all. Just seemed a shame that someone that looks like you might be alone."

"Maybe I'm alone by choice."

I watched his smile deepen as he said, "I could try to persuade you otherwise. Vegas is more fun when you're with someone."

I didn't use any beauty spells to enhance what he was seeing. It had to be true. And a little bit of small talk wouldn't hurt. "Where are you from?"

"Ireland. But I've been here for a while. In the States at least."

"I thought I heard a bit of an Irish lilt."

"I've been here mostly for business. A few years now."

"Where's home?"

"Dublin. Where are you from?"

"California." Where was my waiter? I could really use a sip of a piña colada. It would look more natural to drool after a drink. His stare was mesmerizing as he glanced down my legs.

"What's your business?" I asked as I angled toward him so he could get a better look.

"Dancing." He smiled wide as he leaned back on the lounge chair next to me.

I lowered my sunglasses a bit. "What kind of dancing?"

"The kind where I do a slow removal of articles of clothing."

"You mean stripping?" I took my glasses off. He had just gone up on my interesting scale.

"Well, some may call it that. I think of it," and he leaned closer to whisper, "as a purposeful removal of clothing to create a provocative reaction."

His hot breath brushed across my cheek sending shivers up my spine. I could feel the sweat forming on my body. It wasn't the desert heat. It took me a moment to whisper back to him. "Stripping."

"No," he leaned back a bit dismayed. "There is an art to it. Anyone can strip. But with the right music—" He stood up and started to sway, undoing his cuffs. "—and the right eye contact." Then he smiled and undid a button. He moved his hips in a swivel and undid the other. Some girls started to look at him from the other side of the pool. "You can do a lot."

Warmth was starting to spread to my thighs. He was too tasty to look at.

"So." I swallowed to gain some decorum as he sat back down after nodding to the other girls. "When is your next show?"

"Eight and ten o'clock. The 'Men From Around The World' show at the Hidden Grotto. I'll leave a comp ticket for you at the front window. What's your name?"

I smiled. God, he was good. "Interesting way to get a girl's name."

"If you're not interested, that's fine." He put his hands in his pockets and started to walk away. "It's been nice…"

"Wait. I didn't say I wasn't interested." I felt compelled to convince him to stay. I leaned forward. I was feeling the heat climb up my legs again. "Your strategy worked. It's Catherine Banks." I know this is Vegas, but even here, you don't meet hot Irish strippers every day. "I'll see what I can do. I'm not sure which show I can make."

"The comp is good for either show." His smile lit my fire in more ways than I wanted to admit. "Hope to see you. Off to get some dinner and get ready." He kneeled down and pulled my hand up for a kiss. His lips pressed against my hand, lingering to create tingles down my arm.

"Me, too." I managed to stammer out as my mind went into meltdown mode. I watched him walk away as I heard a familiar Australian accent behind me.

"Who was that?"

I recognized Jeff's voice instantly. Oops. How long had he been there? I tried to play coy as I turned to answer him. "Some guy that wanted to talk." I wasn't going to ask how long he'd been there. "Ready for some food?"

"Yeah. Dinner sounds good." He looked me up and down.

I caught his stare, so I played up my new suit, maybe distracting him a bit further. "I'll have to get out of my bikini first." Hopefully, he'd missed the full scene. I thought if I put on the new black and white dress again, we could get more distracted together at dinner, or after. But, as we left the pool, my mind kept drifting back to a certain Irishman.

# Chapter 2

His reply had sounded dissatisfied with my answer. Damn strange. I'd done nothing wrong. Just a casual conversation with a fabulously gorgeous stripper. There was no crime in that. But then, warlocks were very territorial. Getting past this was going to be a hard sell.

The Stratosphere loomed as we rode in the cab through the section of town known to locals as Naked City. The cab driver seemed to know the nickname for North Vegas but not the reason. Witches have to keep some things secret. Let's just say the real fun can be found in North Vegas. I turned to Jeff with a big smile on my face.

"What's that for?" He asked knowingly.

"Just thinking of why North Vegas can be more fun than the Strip."

"And how much experience have you had there?" He raised an eyebrow.

"What happens in Vegas, any section, stays there. But let's say, I loved the shower room over at that place." I pointed to a strip club I remembered from the not-so-distant past.

We pulled up to the cab drop off, and I threw the driver a twenty. "Keep the change." Rich wasn't the only one with money. But I was footing the bill so far for the trip, and wasn't really sure I wanted to continue this way.

It was hard to know exactly what I was feeling. So much had happened in the last few days. My best friend had slept with my husband. I found Jeff who seemed to be helping me sort through the loss, but then we bumped into the soon to be ex-husband on the way to Vegas. My new boy toy wanderings had been good so far, but very intense. I was starting to lose the rush.

When Jeff came around to help me out of the cab, I asked, "How does the Top of the World restaurant sound?"

"Sure. Haven't been there. Food any good?"

"I enjoy it. But it's the view that matters."

We cut through the casino and headed to the restaurant entrance. First, the maître d' wanted to know if we had a reservation. I asked if there would be room while handing him a hundred-dollar bill. He whisked us past the line and straight into the elevator. Didn't even have to use one spell. It's true that money always talks in this town, sometimes better than a spell.

An old Dean Martin song was playing in the elevator on the way up in the tower. I started humming to "Sway."

"You like Dean Martin?" asked Jeff, his head bobbing to the infectious song.

"When it's one of those real songs, yes."

"Define real."

"In the moment real." He did have a cute smile. I felt him rubbing against my backside as our hips moved to the music in the tightly packed elevator. Maybe there was still some fun left there. But I needed to have no limits. I eased away a bit.

He nodded at my answer as other people crammed around us making small talk until we arrived. The 110 floors flew by, and the doors swooped open; we glided out to the second reservations desk. We were led to our table, right on the bottom of the two-floor restaurant.

I took a seat that gave me the window view, and Jeff sat opposite me. I was hoping the trip in the elevator gave him a clue. Maybe if I hinted about exploring our options, he'd follow along. I looked past Jeff, over his shoulder, and saw all the glories that were Las Vegas: the Strip and downtown. I thought of the possibilities, which included making a certain ten o'clock exotic dance show.

"I wonder how long this takes to rotate once?" I brought my attention back to Jeff and looked into those blue eyes.

He turned to look at the view. "Breathtaking. I could take it in for awhile."

"It rotates once every hour and ten minutes," answered the waiter as he grabbed our attention from the view. He loomed over us with a knowing smile.

"I bet you get that question a lot." I laughed to cover my embarrassment. I tried to cover with a wink up at him.

"All the time. But I always answer with a smile." He had a cute dimple when he talked. Oh dear. I was definitely having a wandering mind. I needed to focus on talking to Jeff.

"Good answer." I skipped to the easiest subject to talk about. "I think I need a good sweet wine." Lubrication always helps the situation. I had a feeling I'd need it; a lot of it.

"Would a rosé do?"

"Yes." I answered with a sigh.

"I'll have a beer." Jeff's Aussie accent was adorable. But his frown of concentration about beer had to be admired. "What do you have?"

"Stout, lager, preference?"

"Your best lager."

"Very good." He handed our menus. "I'll bring the drinks in a moment."

There was an awkward silence after the waiter left. I tried to break it by speaking first. "The view is amazing."

"Yes."

Nothing. I was starting to see that we didn't have much in common, except that we were both witches. I guess the rubbing in the elevator was just some instinct between us. But I had to be honest. This was moving way too fast. Of course, having two warlocks pissed off at me wasn't the best idea either. If I could ease into my feelings, maybe he'd understand.

I looked around, hoping to make conversation about the romantic mood that surrounded us. A quiet classical piece played in the background. A large jungle of ferns separated us from the other side of the restaurant, and plants were strategically placed around the tables, attempting to provide a sense of intimacy. So my people-watching potential was limited to those nearby. Most of the patrons wore varying attire, from business casual to dressed to the hilt, but nothing to really talk about.

At the nearby tables, couples seemed to be sharing their special moments. I would bet the guy at the table to my left was going to propose. He was sweating too much and had a strained smile. Behind us, I could hear a couple cracking up laughing. The couple to my right was older, graying hair to match, each one seemingly comfortable with the other, not needing to talk. There were signs everywhere. Was I ready to be part of a couple again so soon?

I looked at Jeff again. His blond hair fell over one eye. He was spot on with the hard, surfer look. He did clean up well, after a shopping trip for a change of clothes and new leather shoes. The hitchhiking jeans were replaced by tan dress pants. His dress shirt hugged the contours of his chest in just the right places, and I had intimate knowledge of his sculpted abs and what lay below. There was nothing to surprise me now. I smiled at him as I crossed my legs in my black and white dress. Admiring him wasn't making my plan to put the brakes on our relationship any easier.

If I worked the dress right, maybe I'd get his attention in the way I wanted so I could smooth things over. Tight fitting dresses always got attention. I'd added a rhinestone necklace for dinner and high heels that would be worthy of a photo shoot. I licked my lips. It felt good to have a proper lipstick and make up applied. Vegas was a place to let yourself shine, in any form. I could feel his eyes watching my lips.

I let out a big sigh. He tensed a bit. I think he knew something was coming. I decided it was time to just address the elephant in the room. "You know, I've been wondering where this is going."

"Does it have to go anywhere?" He reached for my hand and I let him take it. But I wasn't going to let his luscious body and those blue eyes trap me. I needed space. Darn it. Why was it always a warlock? Why couldn't I fall for a mortal from time to time?

"Well, maybe I need a compass to offer some direction." I bit my lip a little. I didn't want to hurt him, but I had to be honest.

"We can go wherever we want." He tried to draw my hand closer.

"That's what I'm worried about." I drew my eyebrow up. "I'm not sure if I want the 'we' yet."

"Fair enough." He paused and grabbed my other hand, cupping them together. "What do you want?"

I looked into those eyes. They stared back with a sincere need to hear my side. He was open to my opinion. That was definitely a plus. Jeff was willing to listen. I wet my lips again and answered, "Space. Options."

He looked down for a moment. Then grabbed eye contact with me. I held it as I waited for his answer. He started out with a longing in his voice. "I've enjoyed every minute I've been with you. But I can understand why you need space right now. I'm sure it's been a difficult three days."

Now I grabbed his hand. "It's not really you." I looked down searching my mind for the words that wouldn't cut apart his heart. "You've helped me get through some of the tough moments."

I watched his body language for a sign of tension. I gripped his hand tighter, but started to feel his shields coming up. They bounced back against mine. Oh no. Not the best sign. Witches flexing their shields was always a heads up.

He took a breath and answered. "I understand. Just know that I trust you to follow your own path. I've known Rich long enough to know that he'll come back to haunt you at the worst time. Just be on your guard. Know at least, I'd like to keep in touch after all of this."

"Thank you. Time may help, you know."

The waiter interrupted with our drinks. I let go of Jeff's hand. His full shields went up after I did so. Great. I wanted space. I got it. Vegas is definitely the place for everyone to start over. I wasn't in much of a mood to eat, but I had a fantastic view. I looked up at Jeff, then the Strip. It wasn't a total loss.

"I've had a good time with you, Jeff. But space is a good thing for me right now."

"Cat, I'm good with that. We've had a lot of fun together."

I smiled and looked down at the menu. Great. I'd made the awkward moment mammoth. I thought of something to ease the blow. "You can say that again. And who says there won't be some more fun around the corner. For now, let's drink to some badass times together. And maybe when there is less crap going on, we'll continue where we left off."

We clinked glasses. He smiled at me and said, "I'll drink to that." There was a reservation in his actions, but he'd taken it well. After all, with my feelings in turmoil still, I didn't want to drag another warlock into my life. Besides, I kept thinking of a certain dancer. My mind kept drifting to the idea that I might be able to make the ten o'clock show.

"To freedom," I answered. It was what I needed at the moment, and I was glad Jeff understood. "There's only one thing to do now."

He eyed me again. "And that would be?"

I looked at him realizing that there was still a bit of spark in his playful gaze. "Options."

\* \* \*

The witch's lounge was through a small portal of the Chandelier Bar in the Cosmopolitan. Only witches were allowed. I figured it was the best place for us to look for options.

We went up through the casino with the music of a '40s retro band coming from the stage below. I've found most casinos cater to the paranormal crowd. Vampires, werewolves, witches are welcomed throughout Vegas. There are secret alcoves and VIP rooms, and the undead and immortals literally swarm Vegas just because they can. If a buck can be made, any casino has got what you need, especially if you live as long and have as much money as we do.

Most of the fabulous bars in Vegas competed for the paranormal. It was all about access, and witches could sense the spells used to create them. It was a simple illusion spell that didn't allow mortals to see it. Most of the time, mortal eyes would glide over, but we'd be able to see the velvet rope and door.

The Cosmo was no different. They opened their witches' lounge in the secret room adjacent to the Chandelier bar through a spell door. Between the two of us, we should be able to easily gain access past the current blocking spell. Or at least find the portal. It was always tricky finding the right unlocking spell, but then, that was part of the fun. Witches love challenges.

We went up the center spiral staircase that gives a peek through to the casino. I looked down, careful not to slip on the lit stair. A bluish glow lit my ascent. I looked at the chandelier wrapping around the bar with millions of strung crystals woven like a glistening spider web. Holding the metal railing, we entered the lounge area on the second level, and immediately headed to the bar.

I figured this was the place to try a cosmopolitan, switching from my usual piña colada. I'd heard this drink was a specialty here. Everyone was right. The cranberry juice mixed with sweetness hit my senses. It definitely was strong enough to give a witch a buzz. It must knock down humans.

"Just going by the expression on your face, that must be a good Cosmo," Jeff commented as he grabbed another beer.

"They certainly know how to treat witches right. I can feel the kick in this one." I took another sip watching three cranberries bob in my drink. The dimmed lights of the bar lit everything with an afterglow. I lowered my glass, savoring the tang of the juice around my lips with one soft sweep of my tongue. I noticed Jeff watching me as I smiled. "Let's find that portal."

Maybe the tongue thing was unkind and leading him on. But it was such a yummy drink. I couldn't help myself. Besides, I needed to taste new things.

We roamed around the railing that was one of the lounge's chandelier interiors. I sent my energies out to find the portal that would allow us access to the witches' lounge. Feeling a pull, I walked toward the back of the room and saw the portal tucked behind a curtain of crystals. To mortals, it would look like a section that looked out at the casino. But I could clearly see the red velvet rope and gargantuan doorman.

Flipping my hand, I used a basic disillusion spell, and the portal glowed and became completely visible. Any witch in the area would have been able to see it. The security man stood at the velvet rope nodding. "Welcome. Do you have reservations?"

I smiled, and handed him a hundred-dollar bill. "Do we need one?"

He took the bill and smiled. "No. This room is specially reserved tonight for a select group of your kind. Please forgive me for asking. I can make an exception in your case." He gave me a wink and pocketed the hundred.

I saluted with my Cosmo and gave him my best "thank you ever so" look. "It's your job. I understand," I offered as I walked past. No real drama. I liked that.

"Thanks, mate." Jeff took a swig of beer as we walked into the witches' VIP room.

I felt a compulsion spell designed for blocking the senses of mortals to bar their entry, but it didn't have much effect on me. Or was it my drink?

Jeff paused at the threshold for a few moments shaking his head a bit. "That is a strong one. No mortal could get past that one unless escorted by one of us."

Definitely the spell, not the drink then. I sucked down more of the intoxicating beverage, thinking of a possible second. "Must be set by one of the best witches in town."

I perused the room, making a quick search for an empty table. It was indeed a witch gathering of some sort. Women stood about the room in different tones of colors, even ones that were more brilliant to witch vision. I didn't need a black light to see the dresses glow in the dark. Some of the women had gone to dress designers that worked exclusively with color designs for witches' eyes.

But my eye was drawn to the men. Warlocks abounded. I started my sweep into the room, enjoying the stares that were drawn to me. I made my entrance, and Jeff slipped in behind. The gals were already undressing him with their eyes.

"Cat? How are you?" A dark brunette sauntered up to me with a big plastic smile, giving me fake kisses on either side of my face.

"Vivienne." The bitch. She stole my boyfriend in college. But payback is a bitch. I got a chance to get him in my room, where he tried to make moves on me, but I had a camera strategically placed and made sure she was watching on an Internet feed. Their relationship ended with a kick, and Viv and I ended on speaking terms. But I still didn't trust her with any man of mine. I matched her hello with an equal amount of fake, enthusiastic charm. "Seen any good webcasts lately?"

A flash of thunder crossed her eyes for a moment before she could school her face into her most charming. "No, Catherine. I haven't had the fortune to find the time." She turned to Jeff, most likely the reason she came over. "And who is your friend?" She lit up with extra fakeness.

I liked Jeff too much to see him get entangled with that she-devil. She was not good enough for him. So, I covered with a quick intro. "Jeff, Vivienne. We were in the dorms together at college." I took a sip of my Cosmo. Yum. Thank God I had a drink to get me through this. Wow. I was feeling the after effect of extra alcohol. The bartender must have been trained to spot witches and give us an extra spike.

"So, what was Catherine like in college?" Jeff seemed extra coy with the comment.

"She was a darling. Always kept me updated with the classes we shared. Plus, the extra research she'd post to me on webcasts."

She turned to me with a bit of snark. "Cat was such a dear. You always knew how to take care of a warlock." She winked.

"Glad I could help. So, Jeff, let's see who else is here." I tried to pull him away, but he didn't budge. He kept trying to make small talk with just about the worst nemesis from my past.

"Go ahead. I'll catch up." He gave me a wicked smile.

I gave Jeff a little shake of my head. If he wanted to take on Viv, he was asking for it. She always went after guys that I liked. But then, maybe I needed to cut my losses. "Sure." I tried to keep the bitterness out of my voice. After all, I wanted to work on my options, too. "I'm going to check out the room."

Options. That was what I needed to focus on. I moved away from Jeff and started to look around at the available men. They were all warlocks. A small aura of power circled the blond warlock by the bar. A well-built, black-haired beauty of a man was next to him. Of course, that could say one thing, they probably weren't straight. There were a lot of casual encounters for all types going on. I would have to pass on that option.

One warlock caught my eye. He had a tease in his stare that drew me to him. I walked to his raised table and put my drink down. "You drew me over. Most spells don't work on me."

"But I know you too well, Cat." Then, he dropped his illusion spell. Damn it. Rich. My ex-husband. Really? I was starting to wonder why I kept falling for his tricks. "Rich, what are you doing in Vegas?"

"The same thing you are probably doing, forgetting the past." He raised a drink to me. "To moments remembered."

What the hell. It was better than having a spell battle with him. Our resolution of peace had lasted until now. We were in a highly spell-protected witch lounge. He couldn't hurt me here. Well, at least not physically. I raised my glass and downed the rest of the Cosmo. I was definitely going to need another one.

"Where is Jeff?" he asked with a chuckle.

"Over with what the cat dragged in. You remember Vivienne?"

"Oh yeah, and that prank you did on her. I have to say, I think you won." He winked and caught Viv's attention. She saw Rich and darkness crossed her eyes. The room was starting to get too crowded for me.

"Hi, Catherine."

I turned to the perky voice that I'd last heard cowering in my bedroom. Cassandra. I turned slowly. Okay, girl. Remember you were best friends at one time. "Cass." I forced a smile. "You're looking good." After all, I was moving on. All the times we had together, that's what I had to remember now. But I still wanted to scratch her eyes out. She backed up a little.

"I haven't seen you since the night you left Rich. I'm sorry for everything. I wanted to tell you how sorry I was, but then things started flying around, and…." Cassandra backed away from me.

"Cat, you're glowing."

I felt the damper spell hit me. Damn. I had to keep my temper under control. There would be no blasting anyone in here. "I wish I could say I'm over it, Cass, but I'm not. Really, don't piss me off, or I'll blast you to yesterday."

"Catherine, you need to calm down." Rich put a hand on my shoulder. "You're getting looks from security. This is a neutral area. You could get us all kicked out."

"Good, because I'm kind of done with you both." I shrugged his hand off me. "Don't touch me, Rich." I put my glass down on the table. "You can have him, Cassandra. Hope he makes you as miserable as he did me."

I started to storm out, but first went over to Jeff. "I'm getting out of here. Rich is here with Cassandra."

Jeff looked at me, then Viv. "I'm trying out my options like you suggested, Cat." He gave her a long stare.

"Fine, I'm outta here." I was done with warlocks. I walked out of the portal and into the Chandelier Bar's main floor. I wanted to catch a cab quick. I had a ten o'clock show to catch.

# Chapter 3

I tipped the cab driver as he dropped me off at the Hidden Grotto Room, home of the International Exotic Dancer Show, Hot Men From Around the World, and headed to will call to see if my name was on the list. I passed by a poster that had Liam standing next to four other men. My eyes were drawn straight to him. He was the hottest in the picture, with his piercing blue eyes and sexy black hair.

"Hi, I'm Catherine Banks. I've got a will-call ticket for a show tonight."

"Oh yeah." The ticket lady looked me up and down. "Liam put a Catherine on his list tonight. You must be her." Her snarkish tone stung as she printed out a ticket and handed it to me. "You'll love the show." Her grin was ear to ear. "He doesn't do this for just anyone."

"Thank you. Good to know."

Shaking off the weird ticket lady, I entered the lobby, presented the ticket, and headed straight for the bar. There's nothing like a good glass of wine to get you ready for exotic dancers. I ordered a white zin and sipped it as I walked about the room.

Your typical Vegas audience was there. I counted at least five bachelorette parties, with the "Bride to Be" decorated with tiaras, banners, or exotic feather boas. Really, I'm sure it didn't change much each night. Other women were sitting at tables in different attire, from frumpy housewives to hot-as-you-can-handle clubbing outfits. Tight-fitting dresses and skirts were accented with bling on bracelets, necklaces, and rings. You could land an airplane with the amount of sparkle in the room.

Two guys arm in arm walked over to talk to me. "Hi, honey. Where you from?"

"California." I smiled back. They looked like a cute couple.

"We're from LA. We just had our first anniversary. So, we thought we'd come to Vegas to celebrate."

"Has it been a good year?"

"The best," said the other man, eyeing his partner.

"You come for a celebration?"

"Yes. I left my husband. I'm celebrating the freedom."

They both raised their drinks. "To looking for a better man and leaving the others behind."

"I'll drink to that."

The lights started to flicker, and the crowd began to move in the direction of the theater doors. "Show time," said the more flamboyant half of the couple. They headed off in the direction of the doors, and I looked above for my section.

I checked my ticket. Section A, table 4. Hmm. I looked up to find the right door to enter. The crowd gathered together walking through the doors, mixing tiaras, boas, and sparkles. Everyone was hyped for some exotic dancing action.

I lined up next to the door for Section A, and had an usher look over my ticket.

"Oh, you can come with me." He motioned for me to follow. He took me up the middle aisle and showed me to a table in the front next to the center catwalk. I was seated with another group of girls that was just there for a lot of fun. Not one of them sported a "Bachelorette" banner or tiara. These were the girls dressed to the hilt with spangle. I admired their flare.

One of the girls turned to me, her slurring evident of the alcoholic pre-lubrication. "So, you ready for the fun?"

"Sure am," I answered. I took a sip of my wine. "You hear in Vegas for any particular reason?"

"It's my birthday," said the inebriated brunette. The other girls let out squeals of agreement.

One of her friends leaned over to me, "It's about fucking time she celebrated. She's a mother of three and hasn't had a night out on the town that I can remember. Let's hear it for Angela's big thirty-fifth birthday."

The other girls seated around her pulled out some noisemakers and started blowing like crazy. I started laughing. "Happy Birthday, Angela. You so fucking deserve it." The girls at the table started cheering again as a waiter arrived for our drink orders.

"Any more libations ladies?"

Angela went first, her slurring getting more pronounced. "Those margaritas were really good. I think we should do another round of those." All the girls cheered their agreement as the waiter looked to me. I downed the rest of the glass and said, "I'll have another white zin, please."

"Coming right up, gorgeous." He winked at me, and then turned to the ladies. "I'll be right back with your drinks, and maybe a little something extra for the birthday girl." He gave a shake of his hips and the girls responded with a cheer.

The lights dimmed, and everyone broke into applause. The girls at the table started to scream, and I joined them. The energy in the room went up an octave and the audience cheered as shadows took their places on the stage. As the lights came up, men were lined up across the stage with their heads down. Chords come jamming through the loud speakers, and Adam Lambert's voice breaks through with the song "For Your Entertainment."

I was nearly knocked over by the sight of gorgeous men all in tight black silk dress shirts and slacks. Each one did a walk toward the front tables, which got all of the girls screaming. The catwalk center stage extended between our table and another one nearby. My eyes followed the hard bodies down the aisle with each guy until I finally saw Liam.

He did his strut, swinging his hips to the beat of Adam Lambert's voice. He stopped at the end of the catwalk, picking out a girl to connect with as he lowered his body for a grand opening of his shirt. Their screams escalated as he spun and threw his shirt from the stage. I lost my ability to think as Liam started grabbing his belt and pulling it through the loops. He swung it over his shoulder and walked back down the aisle to stand with the rest of the dancers as another came forward to take his place.

I didn't pay much attention to the other man except to notice that he was blond. I was keeping my eye on Liam. He was standing in the back swaying in time with the other men in the review. When the blond man returned to his place center stage in the dance formation, all at once they came forward as the song neared the end.

They stood, in a line, each eyeing a different girl at the front tables. That's when Liam noticed me at my table. We made eye contact as he smiled. I could feel the blush as I returned his look. But quickly covered it with one of my wicked smiles. Hell if I was going to let him see me blush. But, he is intoxicating.

On the same beat, all the men pulled their pants off in unison. The yelling escalated as they held a pose in black speedos, and then everything went dark. My heart was pounding so fiercely I wasn't sure if it was from Liam or just the fact I'd had seen a line of gorgeous, practically naked men in front of me. I figured it was a little of both.

The girls at my table all started talking at once about who was the most good-looking guy. There were no doubts for me. And I waited, heart thumping with excitement steaming my core, for the next time Liam would appear on stage.

It didn't take long. One of the other men of the world performed a solo dance first. He was the hot blond I'd noticed earlier. His theme was a masked warrior, complete with an axe like Thor. He was followed by a Scotsman with wavy, long brown hair. His hair swept over his shoulders as he danced. I was dying to see what was under his kilt. Then, Liam came on.

My heart fluttered nonstop as Liam slowly strutted down the aisle. He was working a James Bond look, complete with a white tux and black tie. A Bond movie theme song blasted from the speakers.

His eyes scanned the room as he walked down the catwalk, looking at one woman; he approached her and went down on one knee, leaning toward her from the catwalk.

He let her undo one of his cuffs. Then he spun around and went down on bended knee to another woman on the other side of the catwalk. She caught on quickly and undid the remaining cuff. With a smile, he stood back up and walked to the end of the riser.

He struck a pose at the end, turned to the side, and worked the jacket down one shoulder, and off the other. Then, he went for the tie. He loosened it, and pulled it out from around his neck, to loud applause. Folding it gently, he stepped down the stairs at the end of the catwalk and presented the tie to the birthday girl sitting at our table.

He moved to another woman at the table and had her stand up. Placing her hands on his chest, he let her unbutton his shirt. Slowly, he pulled it off his shoulders and down off his arms as our table went wild. Throwing the shirt onto the stage, he eyed the table again, and found me. He gave me a long stare.

I couldn't help but wink at him and that seemed to be his cue. The spotlight followed him as he got down on bended knee and pointed to the belt at his waist. I didn't have to be told twice. I reached over and unbuckled it. He pulled the belt from the loops slowly, gently, and lowered it behind my back. All the women at my table squealed with delight. Catcalls were called out around the room.

He pulled me a bit forward, toward his chest. He slid his hand between his pecs, then down his torso toward his waist. Then, he pointed at the crotch button. One of the ladies at our table shouted, "Go, girl."

"Turn that boy free!" yelled another.

I couldn't resist him. I pointed at his chest and slid my finger down his abdomen, then undid his crotch button. He rolled his shoulders and did a slow turn as I grabbed his butt. The whole place went scream crazy as he walked back up the steps to the catwalk. My cheeks were burning red. I could still feel the texture of his chest under my fingertip.

He stopped at the end of the walk, rocking his hips, and pulled one side of the jeans down, then the other. Turning, he bent down, revealing a lean ass covered by a black G-string. Then, he let the jeans fall and stepped out of them.

Turning again, he walked back down the catwalk, bending back, doing a tummy roll, making his abs dance for the lucky lady who was sitting near that side of the riser. He went down on one knee again, and guided her hand to touch his bellybutton. She drew back laughing, and he took her finger, placing her hand on his chest, and guided it down the middle to his abdomen to his G-string. Someone at her table handed her a dollar that she placed under his left hip string. He held her hand there, drawing it back to feel his left buttocks. She erupted with embarrassed laughter, her eyes wide with a grin frozen on her face. She blushed beet red from the experience. I thought she might explode.

He turned to another woman with a raised dollar bill. He dropped down to one knee as she placed it on his other hip string. Several women at my table started pulling out dollar bills, trying to lure him back to our table. One even had a twenty in hand.

He made his way down the catwalk to us again, stepping down the stairs until he was at our table. This time, he went toward the birthday girl. He put his hand out, inviting her to stand up with him, and guided her in a dance move. He placed both of her hands on his chest, guiding them around, and wrapped them behind him.

Grabbing her like a tango dancer, he leaned her back, and then straight up again, looking her in the eye. He pulled her in close and kissed her neck. Our table cheered again as he sat the birthday girl back down, and stepped my way.

He motioned to me in a come-hither way, as I walked up to him. I presented my hand to him and he pulled me in close to him, hard. I banged into him, my breasts pushing up against him. My nipples started to harden at the contact. The place erupted into screams as he leaned me back. I gave in, letting my hair fall and brush the floor. I gave him control of my body.

As he pulled me back up, he whispered in my ear, "I'm glad you came." Then, he gave me a kiss on the neck, taking his time to press his lips firmly on my skin. I closed my eyes, only to realize he'd guided me back down into my chair and was already backing up and turning to go back on the riser.

"Damn, he likes you girl," said one of the women at my table.

The Bond theme song started to replay the chorus, and Liam got back up onto the center catwalk and swayed his hips as the last verse ended. He bent to a pose on one knee and froze. The lights went down and everyone erupted in applause. I found myself saying out loud in the dark, "Holy shit. Who the hell is this guy?"

# Chapter 4

A note arrived at the table just before the show ended. "When the show is over, meet me at the backstage entrance. —L" I'd never wanted strippers to finish a show quickly. This was a first.

As the lights came up, I said quick good-byes to the birthday party gals and made a beeline to the side of the theater where a black curtain closed off the back from the main room. I tried to look nonchalant as a few girls walked past helping each other stumble out of the showroom. I hate waiting.

I was wondering why I felt so on a leash with this guy? If I had a dick, I was definitely being led by it. But I kept wondering about his vibe. It was so intense. I was drawn to him, almost paralyzed. This had never happened before. There was something about this guy. When he looked at me, I went all to jelly. That hadn't happened since college. I thought that was a thing in my past.

I sighed a couple of times as the club continued to clear out. I saw security herding and waving people toward the exits, and some sat at the tables still finishing their conversations and drinks. He'd better show up soon. I was not a waiting kind of girl.

"Hi there. Glad you came." His Irish accent heated my insides as I turned around. He was wearing a black T-shirt and black jeans. Somehow, he made the mundane look chic. I wanted to caress up and down his arms and lift the T-shirt. I wanted more than a peek of what I'd seen earlier.

"Well, good thing you showed up. I was going to give you a few more minutes." I waited a beat to make my point clear. "I don't like to wait around."

"You shouldn't. I just had to get back into my regular clothes and wait for the place to clear out a bit. Come on. I've got to grab my things. Then, we can go."

He pulled me in the backstage area, down a narrow dark hallway into a closet dressing room. "Nick, this is Cat." I noticed the blond Thor from earlier onstage. Well, if I had to have a second pick, at least I didn't have to go far.

"Hi." I put my hand out to shake his. Nick muttered hello and got back to wiping off more make-up while looking in his mirror. "Thanks for helping me out earlier, Liam."

"Next time, just remember to bring that G-string back."

"You guys share G-strings?" I asked intrigued.

"The laundry eats those things. Plus, they do have a habit of disappearing."

"I can see that happening. They're definitely a Vegas souvenir. Those things don't have much material. They're easy to smuggle out in a purse."

Nick's face grimaced in the mirror. I covered fast. "You know, not much material in the back means the front is monstrous."

"You bet, baby." His tone matched his cockiness. "And they cost a lot for that little bit of material. Part of the cost of the job."

"See you tomorrow, Nick," said Liam as he grabbed his duffel.

"Sure, see you later." Nick returned to the make-up removal process.

I gave him a quick wave, and a "Bye, nice meeting ya" as Liam pulled me out of the cramped space. We went back through the black curtain divider and noticed most everyone was gone. The waiters were clearing tables, and the bartender was wiping down the back area as we passed by the main stage. "See you, Liam," waved the waiter that had brought me the note.

Liam waved and shouted, "Thanks, Frank. I owe you for note delivery."

"Oh, you'll pay me back. I'll make you." Liam laughed as we walked arm in arm through the seating area to the lobby. He turned to me, "So, how did you like the show?"

"It was fabulous. I really liked the way you moved your body. You're a finely tuned man, down to every detail, that I could see." I gave him a wishful look as we walked through the box office side door and onto the street. We headed to the back parking lot and to a black convertible Mustang.

"So where are we going?" I raised my eyebrow as he opened the door for me.

"It's a surprise." He hit the button on his key fob, and the car responded with a click.

"Why should I trust you?" I said as I slipped into the passenger seat.

"Because I'm full of surprises. And you want to see what will happen next," he said before closing the door and walking to the driver's side.

As I waited for him to get in, I thought, damn. He was right.

He settled behind the wheel and started the engine.

"After you, then," I said. "You seem to have the plan." It was feeling good to go with the flow. I think the shock of Rich's behavior had awoken something inside. I felt ready for a new man and new adventures. Maybe this man was my new adventure. I was starting to feel like putty in his hands. And I wanted those hands on me. Soon.

We pulled out onto Las Vegas Blvd, hanging a right into traffic. He turned to me and asked, "Have you had a chance to cruise down the Strip yet?"

"Hell no. If you're offering, the answer is yes."

"Then, let's do it proper." He unhooked the convertible's roof hooks, and hit the button to retract the roof as we sat at the light. "This is the best way to see it."

The heat of the desert washed over me. I took in a breath of the dry air and looked up. Lights were everywhere, in sync with the vibe of the Strip. We passed by the Flamingo, the plumes of lights rolling in vibration with the beat of the car.

Liam hit his stereo, and some house music became the theme for the light show we drove past. Women walking on the street yelled at us as we passed Treasure Island and the Venetian. The Forum Shops seem to hold a call of their own for a future outfit.

We got caught at the traffic light by the Bellagio. Suddenly, music blared from the speakers and the sound of falling water made me turn my head to see the start of the fountain show.

"Damn. This light takes forever," mumbled Liam. The whoosh of the water falls in time to a Beatles medley. It created a spray that cooled the air. Lights flicked in the fountains to the beat of "It's A Hard Days Night." The hypnotic rhythm of the water falling and rising relaxed me.

As the light changed, Liam drove forward through the intersection. We started to pass Paris, the witchy Cosmopolitan VIP room, and the Aria. We went under the footbridge of my favorite part of the Strip, leading between the Cosmo and Planet Hollywood. It's like a slice of an outdoor club. I tried not to flashback on the let down that happened earlier in the evening. I could taste the cranberries in the Cosmo again.

The disappointment rose within my gut seeing Jeff with Vivienne. Sheer knives attacked my veins. Then, the shock of Cassandra with Rich. No stop, Cat. I closed my eyes, trying to shut out the world. I opened them again to refocus. Look at the buildings. Enjoy the current views. I looked at Liam. My gut told me to focus on him and the moment. Maybe he could help me forgot everything.

I watched Liam drive and focused ahead, with the sharp lines of the Prada and Louis Vuitton stores flashing beside me. His hair moved slightly as the wind blew past. His sharp nose and cheekbones reminded me of a hawk. He smiled. Yes. The scenery was changing, and always for the better. God, he had a sexy mouth.

New York, New York loomed with its lights of the famous city, and on the left was the green glow of the MGM Grand. We passed by the Excalibur and Luxor. I watched the lights race up and down along the outline of the black pyramid.

We kept heading down Las Vegas Blvd. until we made it to the famous Las Vegas sign, dating back from its glorious heyday of big cars, Frank Sinatra, and the Rat Pack.

"Want your picture with the sign?" Liam suggested as he slowed down for my answer.

"Sure. That will prove I was here."

He pulled into the miniscule parking lot in front of the sign, where a parade of people walked back and forth vying for the best picture vantage point. We parked the Mustang and headed in the same direction. The Vegas sign was lit up in its vintage glory, the heyday of the '50s and '60s road signs. It hasn't lost its class as the most recognized road sign in the country.

"Go ahead, Cat. I'll take it with your phone." Liam reached toward me as I dug through my purse, grabbed my iPhone and handed it to him.

"Where do you want me?"

Liam smiled at my question. "For right now, in front of the sign."

I did a quick jog up to a posing place, and waited my turn for some Japanese tourists to get their souvenir Vegas picture. Then, I ran up and struck a pose, hands up in the air and wiggling my hips as I seized the moment. I saw the flash from my iPhone as Liam shouted, "One more, Cat." This time, I threw my head back in a laugh. Vegas, baby. Fuck the lot of them, Fuck Rich, Jeff, and Vivienne. It was time to live in the now.

"That one was the best." Liam handed me the phone as I left the spot for the next couple to dash in and pose for their moment in front of the sign. I saw myself, head thrown back in a laugh of carefree optimism.

"That really is a moment, Cat. What were you thinking?" Liam looked over my shoulder at the picture.

I felt the wicked grin cross my face. "Vegas, baby. And to hell with everyone else that has tried to fuck with me."

Liam smiled and said, "Amen to that."

He grabbed me around the middle and pulled me closer. "Where to next?"

I leaned up against him and saw the stubble starting to appear on his chin. "I feel like dancing."

"Then, I know the best place for that."

We got back in the car, and we took one of the freeways back past the Strip. The casinos loomed in the distance, lit up like an oasis of excitement and frenzy. Liam took an exit and slowed down to make a right turn into the Luxor garage. He found a spot and parked the Mustang, then put up the roof. I got out and stretched. Damn, it was time to boogie.

I saw some other girls, dressed for their night out, completely engrossed in their girl talk, which stopped when Liam came around from the other side of the car. They gave me a stare down as he grabbed my hand. I heard the click of their heels as Liam drew me away. Unfortunately, we came to the elevator.

As we waited for the elevator to come, the girls rounded the corner in a gush of gab. We were going to have to share the elevator. I hung onto Liam even more. I could feel their eyes eating him up, and the loathing radiating from them toward me. One sidled up and said, "So, what are you up to tonight? Want some more company?"

Liam, a true gentleman, replied, "I've got all the company a man could want right now, but thanks, ladies."

"Sure thing." There was a giggle from the group just as the elevator doors opened. Good thing. I found myself moving toward a forbidden area of using a spell unwarranted on mortals. Down, Cat. They seemed drunk. Maybe a quick aversion spell would send them on their way once they got off on their floor.

They started easing closer to Liam once we got into the elevator. "Aren't you familiar?" one girl asked.

"I'm part of the Men Around the World cast."

"Yeah. You're on the poster." She turned to me. "God, aren't you the lucky one."

I smiled, flipping my hand to launch the aversion spell. "Yes, I am." Now go away.

The doors opened, and we emerged in the line of people waiting outside a velvet rope. Music boomed down the hall, and a line went around the corner. No. I cringed. I wasn't waiting in line with these bitches bugging Liam all night.

Liam let out a quick, "Nice meeting you," and grabbed my hand. We headed around the corner and to the front of the long line. The house music boomed outside as the bouncer nodded to Liam, and we moved through on the VIP side.

We walked through the dark passage and emerged on a dance floor blazing with lights in sync with the music. Go-go dancers gyrated on micro stages that surrounded the dance floor. A sphere of lights and mirrors spun at the center reflecting the laser lights. Alcoves for VIPs lined the upper floor of the club. A series of flat screens lined one wall, and the DJ was positioned below them, using his power to manipulate the music and orchestrate the frenzy on the dance floor. His hands rose in the air, he led the throng of dancers yelling and waving their hands to the beat. I ran to join them. This time, it was my turn to lead. I grabbed Liam's hand and moved forward with the rush of the beat.

I let the music take my body. The thrum of the bass boomed through my bones. I threw my head, tossing my hair to create a dance space. God, I love taking over a space on the floor. I let myself go, waving my hands over my head. Liam enjoyed the show — watching my body gyrate — and stepped in to join me.

He came in close, then reached up and took my hands. We locked eyes as my hips started to move to his swaying. I've always wondered if I could keep up with an exotic dancer. Slowing my movements down, I led with my shoulders, adding my hips to the beat. He mirrored me. I started swaying toward him, and he continued to follow my lead.

The music changed to another beat. I started some foot action, and then committed the dancing sin of looking at my feet. Adding a spin, I froze when I noticed people were backing up. They could sense a couple was taking over the floor space. I focused again on Liam, and took up the rhythm, moving my arms to hit the beat. I felt the moment intensify as he danced with me.

A fog machine poured down a mist that filled the upper part of the ceiling as I took up the challenge again with Liam. We became a movement of energy mirroring each other shoulder to shoulder on the dance floor. I watched the lights flash in his eyes. My focus went to his neck and arms. I moved in closer, and grabbed his hand. This time, he captured my body in an embrace, as if for our first intimate snuggle. I breathed in the sweat around his neck. My hands moved down his back, feeling the wetness beneath his T-shirt. His lips nuzzled the side of my neck.

That was all it took. I felt trapped. I felt the urge to break free. I didn't want another man to take control yet. I'd won my freedom. I wasn't going to let him get me that easily. He was going to have to work for it a little bit more.

I pushed against him, moving him back. Using my finger in a come-hither gesture, I began moving toward the stairs to the second VIP floor. I wanted to see if he'd follow. I was thinking about where to take him. Some secluded corner, where I could dive in for some fun.

As I strutted off the floor looking for a VIP booth, I turned to see if he'd followed me. He had. I grabbed his hand, taking the lead, and felt a rush of power tingle up my arm. A breath escaped as I felt a surge between my thighs. A pull of some kind directed me to lean toward him. But I broke free of the intense feeling.

We were in the section that had special side tables. The upper floors overlooked the dance floor. I moved up the stairs, sending out a search spell for an open corner so I could lead and conquer. I felt a block, knowing a witch or two were in the spaces. In fact, a quick blast on my shields established a witch in the far left part of the club. I smiled. I got it. Territory established. I slinked to an opposite corner, Liam eyed me as I stopped to look back at him. I got a better grab of his hand and winked back. A twinkle in his eye confirmed I had the go ahead.

I found a spot off to the side with a table, a couch, and curtained alcove. I pulled aside the curtain and stepped around the table to the red, velvet couch. Time to find out what Liam felt like without the spotlight. I slid my hands over his chest, going under the T-shirt to feel a smooth, chiselled chest. It was so wicked to feel my way around.

I eased onto him as he inched along my hip. I caressed his neck, feeling the muscles underneath, smelling his masculine scent. I nuzzled the stubble by his ear, drawing my tongue down to outline his jaw. Tasty. The spice of his scent tickled the edge of my tongue. I could literally eat him up. He was extra man-flavored.

I slipped my hands down to his waist and lifted his T-shirt, reaching up to let my fingers run through his silky soft chest hair.

"No. Not here." He caressed my chin. Wrapping his arms around me, he whispered, "I want to be alone with you. But without an audience."

I was starting to build into a frenzy, wanting to completely ravage him. I needed release. "I hate to sound cliché. But should we get a room?"

"I might know a place." He smiled at me stirring my sexed-up buzz. "In the meantime, let's have a drink." He waved a waitress over, her skimpy skirt and low cut shirt the standard Vegas attire for serving. Liam looked at me. "Ladies first."

"I'll take a Manhattan."

She looked at Liam with a smile, then back over to me. If daggers came out of her eyes, I'd be dead. Back to Liam, smile in place, she gave her best, "And for you, sir?"

"Whiskey. Jameson."

She nodded, giving him a bigger smile than before, daggers back at me, and swept away.

Liam leaned back against the couch, and I felt compelled to close in on him. Cuddling up like the pussycat I was, I leaned on his shoulder. I just couldn't keep my hands off his chest. I started to stroke the contours of his pecs through the T-shirt, then down to his abs and back up. I could feel him relaxing under my touch. I lifted my head to catch a glimpse of his face, and he captured my lips for a kiss.

I edged up higher to wrap my arms around him as I turned to straddle him, embracing him between my legs. I was fully mounted on him, pulling his lips in for a kiss as if I needed to breathe him as air. Each time I stopped for a breath, electricity rocked my body. I wanted to take other parts and suck on him hard. Something was coming over me like nothing ever had before. The effect was numbing my reason, and I didn't care. I breathed in more Liam, savoring his bottom lip when I heard, "Will there be anything else?"

I leaned off and tried to straighten my dress. Liam answered, "No, thank you. That should be enough." The waitress deposited the drinks and sulked off. See ya. I grabbed my Manhattan and raised my glass, clinking with his. "You're right. Let's get out of here." I downed my drink and we clasped hands. This time, Liam led us through the crowd toward the exit.

Back on the highway, I leaned my hand out the window, letting it drift up and down, riding the current like a skateboard. I felt far more drunk than I should be. Or was Liam making me feel this way. It was the little girl unleashed, feeling free and happy for the first time since college. No more Rich. My wagon was unhitched. I could be with anybody. For now, that was Liam.

We pulled into the parking lot of what looked like a high-rise condo building, the windows of people's inner sanctums aglow. I turned to look at Liam. "So, 'just the place' is your place?" He gave me a wink, and I sensed that pull once again.

I skipped across the concrete floor, the click of my high heels echoing through the lobby. Liam pushed the button for the elevator, and I noticed the slight dimple in his chin. I couldn't help but reach up and trace the contour.

"What are you doing?" He grabbed my hand with a laugh.

"Getting to know your contours." I smiled, feeling more wicked than I'd felt in a long time.

"What else are you thinking of tracing?" The twinkle in his eye made me laugh. The bell announced the arrival of the elevator.

I grabbed his hand and pulled him in as soon as the doors opened. "A lot of connecting the dots. I hope."

When the doors closed, he leaned against me. His breathing was heavy as I got back to tracing what was becoming one of my favorite body parts of his. Longing to touch that smooth skin beneath his T-shirt, I pulled it up to disappear under the material. I was engulfed in man scent.

As I lifted his T-shirt higher, his hands met mine to help remove the encumbrance. I tossed it across the elevator. I continued exploring every inch, down his lower abs, and back up to his shoulders. He leaned back, inviting me to caress more.

I traced his biceps as I leaned against his chest. The ding of the elevator and doors opening pulled him from my arms. He reached for my hand, and I let him pull me down the corridor. I want Liam. I wanted him more than anyone before. He was an itch that needed to be scratched. I let him lead me, knowing that I'd soon be allowed to ravage him. I was close to taking him in the hallway, but carpet burns are a bitch.

After a brief fumbling with his keys, we were in. Silence is the unspoken language of shared desire. In that silence, I chose to switch roles. I was now his toy. He pulled me closer, and I slammed myself into him with force. I was ready to play now. I was tired of leading and being let down. I wanted someone to take me now. He took my head and pulled my face toward him. The kiss was firm. Powerful.

He picked me up and took me to his bedroom. "You can throw me on the bed if you want. I'll bounce you know."

That made him laugh. His aim was true, and I landed square in middle of the soft white comforter. Liam followed, gliding over the top of me. I felt the wetness between my legs, anticipating him being inside me. His hands started to push up the bottom of my dress. He stroked my thighs as warmth broke out between them. But then I felt a drain of my energy. It was small at first, and then a burst of force stole my strength.

That's when it hit me. The full force of the lock spell held me down as he leaned over me. I couldn't move. He started to levitate above me, pulling energy as hard as he could. This was worse than a warlock. It was worse than a vampire He was taking too much too fast. I was going to pass out if I didn't stop his energy drain.

I slapped a force spell at him. But he was prepared for that. He smacked it away as he continued to drain me. My hips lifted up toward him as he moved above me, arms outstretched as he continued his drain. This was much worse than warlock imprisonment. There was only one creature that could drain a witch this fast.

"Succubus," I moaned as the strength of his spell pulled me closer towards him above the bed. The energy draining from me was turning me into an organism that would result in my death. I knew I was in trouble, and had to pull free.

But I wanted the final release. I wanted it with all my being. But I knew it would give him the rest of my life force, and the remaining energy would be drained slowly from a death embrace as I slid lifeless from his arms.

I had to focus to survive. I closed my eyes and concentrated. What image would hold me together and give me the strength to fight Liam? There was one face that appeared in my mind: Jeff. His face, his blue eyes, his blond hair, and rugged jaw line. His chiselled nose and smile. His smile. I focused on his smile. The dimple that was to the left of his mouth. Kissing his mouth, over and over. I could feel the strength returning to me. The energy drain began to slow.

I felt the pull losing strength, and I was slowly lowering back toward the bed, away from the monster hovering above. Finally, the power drain stopped. That's when I pulled so hard on my own energy. I hit Liam with everything I had, smacking him against the wall and holding him there. I kept him in check, shielding any energy sources he might have had in his apartment.

"Don't you ever fuck with me like that again," I said, giving him a threatening glare.

"You can't blame a boy for trying."

I threw him up against another wall, looking away, knowing that he could ensnare me into his energy draw again with a single gaze. I had to remain in control and get the hell out of here. If any witch had an enemy, a succubus would be it. And he was a damn good one. I'd fallen for his trap.

"Okay, you know I can flatten you right now. But I think it would be best just to part ways." I flicked my hand to throw more pressure against his neck. "Do we have an understanding that I'm leaving now, and you're not to follow?"

"Whatever you say now, Cat. We could still have a good time. I'll back off the drain a little." Again, I sensed his attempt to pull me in.

Oh, he was good. But never trust a succubus. "Sorry, I never get involved with those that try to kill me. Consider the blue balls you'll have from this as a reminder to not mess with a witch again."

"But you're so tasty. All that energy ready to...."

I continued the squeeze spell on his neck.

He squirmed, "All right. I'll promise safe passage. Just put me down."

I backed out of the bedroom, keeping him pinned against the wall, making sure he felt like a fly ready to be squished. He probably would deserve that, but he might leave too big of a stain.

I got to the apartment door and backed out, leaving the spell intact and set so I could make it down the elevator.

The ding interrupted my thoughts, and I scrambled to the safety of the elevator. I half expected Liam to follow. But he didn't. I was torn between escape and him dashing down to grab me up again, kiss me, and throw me back on his bed. Down girl. You did the right thing. Death by succubus is not pretty.

The doors opened and I walked into the building's lobby. I sent out a search spell, drawing the closest taxi to me. I knew the spell on Liam would hold for a bit longer, but I kept looking at the elevator, expecting him. That need to return to him was pulling hard.

Damn, he had one hell of a draw for a succubus. I'd never had one so strong near me. Shaking my head, I knew I had been stupid. I'd let my guard down. But one thing remained clear, Jeff's face had focused me. That was telling. I hadn't expected encountering a succubus any more than I'd expected my attraction toward Jeff to save me.

The taxi honked at that point, drawing me out of my thoughts. I stepped out of the lobby into cool, dry air. The desert was always the right temperature in the middle of the night.

"Where to?" asked the driver as I opened the door.

"The Venetian." We pulled out of the driveway toward the Strip. I noticed the glow starting over the hills in the distance. It was clearly later than I thought, and the sun was starting to rise. A thought hit me like a target. Jeff. What the hell was I going to say to him?

# Chapter 5

I was all prepared with my excuse as I slipped the card key into its slot. I had needed some time to myself. I was trying to clear my head. I'd just leave out the part about the succubus stripper.

I opened the door and looked to the bed. It was made. Shit. Where was he? I walked around the room; checked the bathroom. I checked through the whole suite. Nothing. I went and slumped on the couch and looked at the view of the Strip. The lights lit up like a spine through the center of Las Vegas, giving it structure and life. Out there, somewhere was Jeff. Where the hell was he? And why did I care?

I guess the question was, did I? Did I really care for Jeff? He was becoming more than just the supposed one-night-stand plaything I'd intended. The problem was, how much did I care? The muddled feeling was gone. I had no stripper to pounce on. That had gone terribly wrong.

But Jeff. He might be something, and it was starting to worry me. I settled back into the couch, cradling a pillow, looking at Vegas at my feet. I had my freedom, and I was starting to think that maybe I wanted to share it, with Jeff.

I must have nodded off for a bit. I awoke when I heard the card key click, and the room door open. I sat up and watched Jeff walk silently into the room.

"Where have you been?" God, was that the jealous girlfriend tone in my voice? I blinked at the sunlight flooding the room.

"Out." He turned into the bedroom part of the suite as I got up and followed him, still holding the pillow from the couch. "I didn't mean it like the jealous girlfriend." There, that was a good cover. I hope he bought it. "I was concerned. You know?"

He gave me a crooked grin. "I'm sure. And when did you get back?"

"Not long ago."

"Trying out your options?" He attempted a smirk, but this time, his gaze was full of hurt.

I didn't answer right away. The puppy-eyed stare melted my insides. I didn't really expect what came out of my mouth next. "Jeff, I don't want it to end like this. Truth be told, I was thinking of someone else all night." And it saved my ass.

"Did you figure out who that was?"

"Are you implying that I'd want to go back with Rich? Hell no." I pulled the pillow closer.

"Well, you did say you wanted to try your options. You are still technically married to him until your vows end. Isn't that soon? People can change their minds. We are in Vegas, the wedding capital." He kept his eyes on me, waiting to make sure I met his gaze. "I'm just waiting to see what you decide."

"Really. I don't want to go back to Rich. He's still an asshole. Always will be. I've tasted freedom, and I like it."

"It sounds like there might be an 'and' after that statement."

I hesitated. Yes. There was. But why? "I'm not sure if someone I've known for a just a couple of days is the right one for me." I moved closer to Jeff. His eyes penetrated my heart. I rubbed up to him as he wrapped his arms around me. "I've been so muddled these last few days. The fact that you're friends with Rich is a dagger to my heart." There, I'd said it. Something released in the air when I spoke. The tension melted between us. Rich had become a barrier. Talking about it—acknowledging it—was breaking it down.

He pulled me closer, his breath moving past my ear as he spoke. "I don't mind giving you space. This is a lot to go through, and I've known Rich a long time, too. You're right, he is an asshole."

The laugh felt good. My tension melted as I snuggled up with him. "You know, before you came in, I was admiring the awesome view from our room. So much must happen down there, and we're witnessing it from above, like deities watching pawns move about. Vegas is a live-in-the-moment kind of town."

He leaned in and captured my lips in a moment of intense, sincere tenderness. It wasn't like our previous kisses. Something had changed.

He smiled in response. "I think I want to live in the moment right now."

We moved to the couch, and I lay down as he wrapped his arms around me. I felt like I could melt into him. His breathing caressed my neck, making the little hairs rise and tickle. My head fell back under his chin, and he pulled me closer. I felt an unleashing of something inside me. I turned in his arms and nuzzled up to his face. His lips brushed against mine.

"I'm sorry. Something snapped inside when I found out you knew Rich. It felt like a betrayal."

"I wouldn't intentionally hurt you, Cat." I was drawn toward the softness of his voice. "I'm finding that I want something more than just our pleasure."

I looked into his eyes. I saw the hope, the wonder. Could I go there again? Another warlock? After the parade of warlocks before him, could I let myself be taken over with that powerful emotion of falling for another?

He broke the spell of doubt by saying, "I need more than just our bodies. I'd want us to join souls."

His words sparked the flame inside me. It had been there, sparked by Liam, but needed the right man to fan it. In that moment, I knew Jeff was the warlock I needed.

I fell upon him like a bitch in heat, drawn by the need to have him again and again. I sucked up his lips as if they were air. He was more than just a one-night stand. He was becoming the warlock for me.

He returned the intensity of my kiss, wrapping his arms around me, our desire pulling from within, as we wove a spell to connect us both. Our bodies continued to move together as we kissed to draw our energies as one.

Finally, I came up for air. "Take me, Jeff." I sat up, pawing his chest, wishing that the T-shirt was already thrown onto the floor.

"No more doors closed between us, Cat." I nodded, and he sealed the promise with another kiss. With that, he pulled me with him from the couch, swung me into his arms, and carried me to the bedroom. And not a moment too soon.

He lowered me onto the comforter, leaning in for a stabilizing kiss. My head touched the pillows, cushioning some of his weight as he closed the gap between us. He moved my skirt up my thighs. A shock moved up my leg as he let his energies push around me.

"You don't need any spells to seduce me, Jeff. I'm yours."

"Oh, I wasn't planning them to seduce you. More of a simple play around with you."

I felt pressure all around me; stroking and caressing my sides, then up my breasts. Then, I lifted up before him, cradled by a force coming from Jeff's hands. I rose into the air as my dress came over the top of my head. I forgot how much fun sex could be with pressure spells.

"Where would you like me to push next?" His touch raised the heat between my legs.

Twisting off my panties, I sent a force spell to have him rise above me. I gently pushed against his chest. He closed his eyes, as I sent a push spell to move his T-shirt over his head. Yum. Jeff hovered over me, my control over his body complete as I directed the energy to search around his skin. I saw the goose bumps rise on his torso and arms. I lowered him down as I rolled out from under him. I wanted to do the honors of removing the rest of his clothes.

I rotated him onto his back and stood above him. Naked. I leaned over him and stroked down his abdomen, grabbing the waistline of his pants. Gently, I unzipped and pulled down the black dress pants. Before me lay a hot, naked warlock, putty in my hands.

"Jeff?"

"Yes." His voice had a roughness that taunted the witch inside me to pounce.

"Get ready for one hell of a ride."

"I'm already with you on that one." He arched his back as I pulled down his briefs. His hard member popped out ready for my attention. My wetness was becoming acute. I needed release as much as he did. I straddled him and pushed against his erect rod, taking him in one large push until I held him right where I wanted him. Each thrust brought shivers up my thighs, until I enfolded him completely.

I unlocked the pressure spell, but he didn't move. I had him trapped by more than just a spell now. I gently rose up and down, stroking with my inner being, the place that was most dear to any warlock. Our pleasure came together as the spells for our soul joining rushed to meet. In that moment, I realized I had found the right warlock.

~

# Never Cross A Warlock

Beware of Warlocks, Book 3

# Chapter 1

"What would you like me to concentrate on today?"

I lowered my face into the little hole in the headrest of the massage table and let out a small groan. "If you could rub out those knots in my back, that would be great."

Yes, there was only one place to go when things were rocky with any man, especially if that man just tried to kill you. The spa. The key to solving all of your problems, or at least to get to that Zen moment of realization, is to get a full spa treatment.

That's how I found myself at one of the best spas in Vegas—face down on a massage table, trying to achieve some kind of relative state of peace to figure out how to deal with my current man problems.

I exhaled as my masseuse rubbed out an especially tight knot. "You have a lot of tension in your back." The masseuse's voice sounded concerned as she used her elbow to release that difficult knot.

"Tell me about it. I can sum up why with one word: warlocks."

She chuckled and gave extra attention to the knot on my shoulder. "I hear you. Just takes one warlock to ruin your balance."

"In my case several."

"Oh, that's a problem to have." She laughed and rubbed down my back in small circles. The smell of the lavender oil created a cloud of forgetfulness.

"I figured a spa trip would give me the Zen frame of mind to sort it all out."

"You've come to the right place. How much pressure do you need?"

"Heavy. Enough to rub out my memories."

She answered with a rigorous attack down the back of my thigh, moving in a smoothing line down my hamstring. I was put into a spell of bliss. I'd asked for a massage specialist for witches, and I could sense the healing energy running through me. God, I needed this.

I let her work me over, the scent of lavender joined by rosemary as she eased my tired, battered muscles—and with them, my emotions—into some sort of balance.

My mind started to wander as her magical hands kneaded out my kinks. If only she could rub out the kinks in my heart. Jeff, my current large knot of a warlock, was better than I imagined. Thoughts of him had actually saved my ass from the succubus stripper that had attacked me last night.

Yet, I was still feeling that non-committal vibe—again. I just didn't want to jump into something right after the huge betrayal my ex-husband was laying on me. Well, soon to be ex. If we didn't renew our vows by tomorrow, we'd be officially split. The only other alternative was a quick divorce witch-and-warlock style. Meaning, I'd have to hide so he didn't try to kill me.

Trust me. Never cross a warlock. Divorce for us was usually a lightning bolt to the forehead. Whoever has the fastest spell blast at the other wins everything. TILL DEATH DO YOU PART is literal in our case.

I sighed as she applied some gloriously painful pressure in the middle of my back. If I were a kitten, I'd be purring. Sometimes, a good rub down brought everything you needed to face into greater focus. And I definitely had a few things I had to sort through. Before tomorrow, I had to decide whether to leave Jeff behind or take him with me? If I chose him, he'd probably get attacked, too.

It could be the reason why I saw Rich in the Chandelier bar last night. He brought Cassandra along to Vegas to bait me into attacking him. If I'd blasted her in the bar, I'd have had half of the Vegas witch squad holding me hostage until Rich had time to set a trap. The squad was always on the alert for rampant displays of witch powers. It could expose us all. Damn. I almost fell for it.

Not to mention Liam. Clearly, a deadly distraction. An Irish exotic dancer, Liam had me going with his incubus skills of draining magical essence. I should have recognized it, but then, it had been a while since I'd seen one. Last time in college, I'd had Viv to save me. Now, I just needed to focus on Jeff and break Liam's spell before he sucked my energy dry. I was going to have to be more careful.

Looking on the positive side, I could've been dead now. But I was still alive. I took a deep breath in and out, and focused on the spa's piped-in music. Native American flute music combined with gentle guitar, soothing my mind. I tried deep breathing as the masseuse rubbed out my arms, wobbling them to align my strained muscles, and then gently putting each one back at my side.

I must have fallen asleep, because before I knew it, she was shaking me softly.

"Okay. I'm all finished. Just move slowly as you put your robe back on. I'll be waiting outside for you."

"Sure. Wow. I think I nodded off. You're good. Thanks."

"You're welcome." She glided out the door.

I revived my relaxed self, remembering to slowly ease off the table and lower one foot to the floor, then the other. I felt so beyond problems. All I had to manage was getting my robe on and slipping on flip-flops to get to my next appointment, a facial. If nothing else, I was going to be relaxed at the end of this. I could deal with everything that awaited me, one problem at a time.

\*\*\*

I emerged into the Las Vegas sunshine, sunglasses affixed, reborn. Spas make all your problems seem conquerable. Jeff waited for me just outside the front door. I'd begun to notice he's considerate in that way. He had been growing on me ever since our first meeting on the highway. What had started as a break-up plaything had been turning into something more. I was still not sure where this was all going, but the possibilities were enticing.

Seeing him now made me wonder why I'd doubted we had any future for us the night before. But then, that was before the succubus had tried to kill me. Now, all I wanted was to pull off his T-shirt. It defined his chest in places I wanted to reclaim from this morning. Memory of his torso began to awaken my body. His black sunglasses set off his blond hair, but hid those amazing blue eyes. Those eyes I wanted to stare into again while making love. He stood in front of me dressed in tight jeans. Memory of this morning's intimate encounter was heating up different parts of me. It took great restraint on my part to keep me from jumping him right there on the street.

"How was your afternoon?" he asked as I went up and settled for giving him a big kiss. After all, we were still in public. "It must have been good," he said after we came up for some air.

"I've been sorting myself out. A lot has happened over the last few days."

He nuzzled up next to my neck in response. Oh yes. He was a keeper.

"I'm guessing you've been thinking about the big divorce proceedings. When is your one-year anniversary?"

His Australian accent made certain parts of my body vibrate. I had to concentrate to answer, ignoring the need to have him stroke his hands down my body again. "Tomorrow, I'm afraid." I swallowed, trying to steady myself.

"It does mean we'll need to make sure we're out of town by today. If he traps you here, I'm sure he'll finish you off."

Jeff hailed a cab as I thought about his point. Did I want to run for the rest of my life? Or was I going to finally stand up to Rich? I just had to be strong. Rich did have an upper hand in clever spells, but I could use Jeff as an ally to send me the power I needed. I could beat Rich. Or could Jeff and I both die? Was I willing to ask Jeff to stand with me?

Confusion contorted my face. Jeff couldn't help but notice as he opened the door to the cab. "Did I say something wrong?"

"No, Jeff. You're the only thing that is right in my life right now." The surprising thing about what I said was that I meant it. It scared me as much as the impending spell battle. Witches had it simple. The strongest witch wins everything. No need for any mortal divorce. I'd have to win or find some other way to get out of it.

He ran behind the cab and joined me on the other side. "What should we do, Cat?"

"Make a plan. Where's a good place to gather resources?"

"Somewhere neutral, I'd imagine. Where's the best witches' club?"

"The VIP lounge at Haze."

"That's the place we'll figure our next move, then." He looked up at the driver. "The Aria."

He turned to me with a new confidence that made me wonder what he had in mind. "We might be able to find some allies, as well. You may not be the only one that is pissed off at Rich."

"Rich has other enemies?" I asked, a bit surprised.

He chuckled at my comment. "He sure does, babe. I think you'd have to get in line behind several other people, including me."

The cab eased out of the back drive of the Venetian behind the casino. I relaxed in my seat. "That's the best idea I've heard yet." I flipped my hand to straighten out the wrinkles in my dress. Cabs were notorious for creating them. I wanted to make a fabulous entrance after all.

"You'd think a woman just walking out of a spa would be more relaxed?" He eyed me with a smile.

"Most women don't have a soon-to-be-ex-husband that can blow her to bits. Well, most of those exes might want to, but mine can." I bit my lip before I went on. I looked at the plastic between the driver and us. Still couldn't risk talking openly about the situation in earshot of the cab driver. It caused an awkward silence as we navigated the back roads behind the casinos to the Aria. Luckily, we didn't have a chatty driver.

When we arrived, I slinked out my side of the cab; Jeff paid the driver, then came around and reached for my hand. As we crossed the lobby, my heels clicked on the marble floor. I admired the sleek, modern style of the hotel. Angles and curves met in stone and paper sculpture throughout the lobby where Old-school shapes and colors of the '60s wove into edgy twenty-first-century glitz. I tried not to stare as we negotiated our way into the adjoining hall that would lead us to the nightclub Haze.

"We might need to catch dinner before it opens. I think I know a place so I can call a few friends."

Hope started to seep into my heart as I heard Jeff talk with such confidence. No one had ever taken on Rich with this much self-assurance. But he'd faced him before. My thoughts must have shown on my face. "I put up with Rich's crap back in the day way too much, Cat. When I last saw him, there was no evidence of any lingering friendship."

We turned into one of the restaurants off of the casino and got in line for a table. "I'm thinking I need to hear the full story of how you know Rich. In fact, there is a lot I want to know about you, Jeff. And probably more you should know about me. I don't want to see you get blasted on account of me, when you really don't know me well enough to take on such risks." There. It was out now.

He reached up to my face and caressed my cheek. "You're concern is well warranted. But I've taken him on before, Cat. And I won."

I couldn't help it. I laughed. The first good laugh I'd had in several days. "Seriously, I would have liked to be a fly on the wall for that."

"It would have been a treat if we hadn't been in the desert at the time. Blowing up Sydney wasn't an option. So, we took it out of town, of course."

"Witch's policy. But what did you do to win?"

"I kept my cool. Push the right buttons on Rich, and he'll go down in flames." Jeff's smile was just too evil to be real. But it made me smile in return. For the first time since I'd high-tailed it out of our mansion, I had hopes of screwing over Rich and finally surviving our witchy divorce. I pictured me dangling him like a spider, pulling off one leg at a time. Okay, maybe not that much of a screw over. But he totally deserved it. A girl could dream.

# Chapter 2

We were shown to a cozy table for two with a stark, dark marble top and flat-backed chairs. I felt tired all of a sudden. All I wanted to do was slump and relax. A spa will do that to you. But I needed to drink more water and eat a healthy meal to get my strength up. Facing an impending spell battle required a witch to be a full spell-casting capacity. Food most likely would help.

We looked over the menus for a few minutes, but then I couldn't take it anymore. "So, what were his buttons?"

Jeff continued looking over his menu. He didn't answer me, and I let the impatience slip out in my voice. "Well?"

"Patience, Cat. I need to eat first. Then, I'll tell you everything. I promise."

His wink was reassuring, but indecision about him still managed to creep into my mind. I still had my worries about making it through this whole ordeal. Was it my lack of confidence in him? Or maybe I just didn't have confidence in myself.

Spell battles happened often enough that witches and warlocks always had to be in shape for such occurrences. But few opponents survived the frays unless there was a truce. I had to know how Jeff had trapped Rich into one.

I watched his eyes glance over the menu. I looked over the menu of American cuisine that tempted my appetite. Then, I decided on something simple. Steak. I could imagine I was cutting up a certain warlock that had it coming. I wasn't the killing type of witch. But removing certain parts one at a time to make Rich squirm was tempting. Just too tempting. But then, I didn't want to lose any of my important body pieces, either. I was rather attached to them.

I put down my menu and wiggled my nose in impatience. "Do you know what you want?"

Slowly, he put his menu down. "Yes," he said, folding his hands on top of the menu and looking up to find the waiter. Damn. I hate waiting. I flipped my hand to ease into a Hurry Spell for the waiter to guide him over, and Jeff blocked me. I gave him my WTF look. "Patience, Cat. Let the waiter come over in his own time."

I gave a bit of a huff. My hair flipped up at the puff of air. I waited. And waited. The frustration built until I almost flipped my hand into a spell to speed up the waiter. But I didn't want Jeff to win this battle of wits.

After a few more of my sighs, the waiter finally made his way over to us. He took our order and our menus. That's when Jeff started to smile again. "Horrible isn't it."

"What?" I answered with another sigh.

"Waiting. That's the answer to your question. What are Rich's buttons. Waiting creates frustration, which can make him mess up his spells. Add some good old-fashioned anger, and we should be able to put him off balance. The thing to remember is to remain calm and have patience." He grabbed my hand and traced circles on its back. "The real question is can you do that?"

I felt tingles going up my arm as he turned my hand over and continued making small circles across my palm. The caress felt comforting and grounding. I felt a wave of balance and strength wash over me. " I think so."

"You have to do better than think so. You have to know so. He's strong, but Rich can be unbalanced if you wait him out. He hates it."

"I know what you mean. He's so impatient, he's pushy to the point of annoying. I'm glad I won't have to put up with it anymore." My revelation allowed me to see a possible end to my prison term with Rich. I could finally be free. Just winning one pesky spell battle to the possible death would be it. Then, we would be done, forever. Forever is a long time for a witch.

"If you think about it, we are people that have been close to him. Maybe too close. He'll hate that, too. But I imagine he's working on some kind of strategy, as well. But we definitely have something that, if worked right, can beat him."

"And that is…"

"Us."

\*\*\*

I hesitated and looked over my drink as Jeff went across the room to meet up with another warlock. We were in the VIP Undead Underground room at the Haze. Some places in Vegas hosted the paranormal guests in mixed company. Vampires walked among shifters and witches. Even mortals were allowed. The mortals had no idea what company they kept.

Music boomed on the dance floor as I watched Jeff and the other warlock walk toward me. The other warlock was cute in a boyish way. He had brown, wavy hair and dark features. He reminded me a lot of Benedict Cumberbatch.

"Cat, this is Tristan Barkley. He's a warlock from the UK. He might be able to negotiate some needed spell battle rules."

He stretched out his hand and I took it. His handshake was strong and sure. "Yes. Good to meet you, Mrs. Banks. I think we can set some guidelines to make it more of a fair fight. Witches fighting warlocks is always a risky battle. A fair judgment on tactics will reduce your risk." His British accent seemed clipped, stressing important parts of the words.

"So, you're a witch divorce lawyer?" I blinked at the thought. A referee might make Rich behave with more civility. But I doubted it would keep me in line when I really wanted to blast him to bits with a fireball spell.

"It does help to have rules set," Jeff added. "They are determined based on your abilities, so it's a fair fight, and a limit of how much damage will be allowed is set to keep the battle from getting too ugly."

"I also can help with dividing up your properties and holdings before or after the battle. It will depend on what your ex-husband agrees to. Of course, there is a clause that if you should renew your vows with him, this would all be over." The Brit looked at me with a baiting stare, eyebrows raised, as if I was some silly girl who hadn't made a decision on my own before.

"No, I'm sure she's finished with him," Jeff quickly answered.

"I do need to hear it from her. That will be the reason to set up the battle. Do you plan to renew your vows with Mr. Banks or not?"

I looked at this guy as he studied me carefully. I wasn't sure who had ordered the Spanish Inquisition. "I thought you were here to help me."

"I am. But I need to be assured of what you really want to do. If there is even a chance of reconciliation, I need to pursue that path before agreeing to the destructive ending of your marriage."

He stopped for a moment and raised his hand to his chin. "But of course, should you choose to say your vows with someone else that day, it would annul your vows with Mr. Banks."

"Really? It could be that simple?" The shock of the answer made my voice rise as high as a schoolgirl's.

Jeff interrupted, "And what would this do for the person she marries. Would he be at risk?"

"Yes, he would. But even if no vows are said, at least she would have someone at her side. Any allies would be a good idea. But then, if Mr. Banks chooses someone to support him, she could take part, as well, if she's a witch."

I let out a big sigh. "Well, Cassandra is a mortal. She would be no good to him except for bugging the crap out of me."

"There is one more thing." Jeff cut in with some urgency in his voice. "If the battling witches can have friends stand up and support them, rules must be established to set a limit of what support can be used."

"Yes," answered the Englishman. "I would highly recommend a limit of who can support. Allies can really give strength to one side or the other. Balance must be kept. Too much ally support can ruin a witch's chances of winning."

"Or like, they'd be dead if not enough people are able to help them." I was getting the feeling I wanted to hide somewhere.

"What about the marriage part?" asked Jeff.

"Yes," I answered reluctantly.

"What if we say our vows? If we got married, we could fight as true allies. Nothing could bar us from the battle. We are already soul bonded." At that, I felt a flutter in my heart as I could feel his closeness to me in the room.

"What if we had a ceremony, got hitched, and then faced down Rich. As a team, we could do it."

I started to imagine us at one of the cute, little Vegas chapels. All good stories end with a wedding, right? But did I want to face the same problem with Jeff one year from now?

"This is a lot to think about." My voice came out so serious; it even deflated Jeff a bit.

"Right. I'll leave you to it, then. It's a decision you'll both have to make. The vow bond is a type of spell, as well. If you state your vows with someone else at the same time the bond has ended with Rich, you might be able to avoid the battle."

An idea dawned on me. "Would Rich try to stop that?" Maybe Rich was already trying to. I was feeling really pushed into something. Trading one warlock for another? Was that really wise?

"The bond must be heartfelt. If you've joined souls, you've already set part of the bond. The link is there. A marriage bond will complete what you've already started." The Englishman raised his eyebrow. "I imagine you've already got an answer. You just have to figure out what that is."

He raised his drink to Jeff. "Good luck to you. I'll contact you both later, once you've had some time to talk this over."

I watched the other warlock walk away as I turned to Jeff. Was I really ready for another wedding vow? Three days after finding Cassandra with Rich, and I was staring down a whole new path.

"Well, Cat, what do you want to do?" Jeff looked me at expectantly. "We've sealed things physically. Mentally, are you ready?"

Good question. Was I?

# Chapter 3

I did the only thing a girl could do when faced with a whole new life. "I need to go to the bathroom. I'll be right back." I slid out of my bar chair faster than I'd ever made an exit. I had to regroup. Nothing like a quiet bathroom stall to clarify your thoughts.

I made it through the bathroom door and stumbled into an empty stall. Sitting on the toilet, a stream of tears burst forth. Once I started, I couldn't stop. I let it happen. Nothing like a good purge to get some sense back into a girl. Was I really ready for a life with Jeff? I felt the soul binding telling me he was the one to stick it out through thick and thin. But then, I thought so with Rich, too. But he'd never done the soul-binding spell. Just the marriage spell, and then we went on a shopping spree, buying houses, cars, and anything else that he thought my money, and now his, could buy. I was so stupid. He was such a cock suck up.

I heard a knock on my stall door. "You okay in there?"

I snuffled, using some toilet paper to clean up the snot from my nose.

"Yeah. Men suck." I wouldn't say warlocks. This was a mixed club.

"I agree with you there, girl. Just let me know if you need something."

I blew my nose a couple of times, wiping off any excess, then stood, straightened my dress, and flushed all the tissue down the toilet. There. My man tears were spent. Time to move on and try to make a decision. I opened the stall door and saw the attendant ready to hand me a towel.

I added a quick "Thank you" before dabbing at my streaked make-up. I was going to have to do some reapplying.

"Sometimes this is the best place to come and let it all out, dear," added the attendant.

"I'm totally embarrassed," I said as I tried to make something out of my raccoon eyes. I'd just gone old-fashioned tonight. No added spells instead of make-up. I liked going all natural, as I called it. I really didn't need spell enhancing, and was proud of that. Not every witch could claim to have a spell-free appearance. I started going through my purse for items to reapply and make better the mess on my face. My brown hair kept flopping in front of my eyes. It was getting distracting.

"Don't be. I get a lot of woman crying out their man problems in here."

"Hear any good solutions?" I started to reapply some liner, giving up on the mascara. I figured just adding more base and rouge would make me presentable again.

"Yes. Most of the answers involve kicking the scoundrels out of their lives, or forgiving them. I'm guessing one of those options might fit yours."

"It does in one case." I laughed. Throwing Rich out of my life would seem fit, if I lived through his retaliation. "I think getting rid of him is the best option." I smiled at the thought of it.

"Oh, girl, two men. That's always a problem." The attendant smiled, leaving me to my make-up repairs. Just then, a toilet flushed and the stall opened. In the mirror, I recognized the woman exiting. It was Cassandra.

I wasn't sure how much she'd heard. She came up to the sink next to me, rinsing her hands. My lips pursed, and I tried to play it coy. I looked in the mirror to touch up my rouge, but I saw my cheeks were plenty red without it. Maybe she wouldn't notice it was me.

"Cat?" Her voice actually sounded surprised.

Shit. "Cassandra?" I tried to put on one of those hated fake smiles. "Imagine seeing you here!"

"Yeah. This is a surprise. Rich and I are staying at this hotel. After the Chandelier Bar experience, we were trying to find you and apologize. Really. It wasn't a thing Catherine. It felt like I couldn't say no to him."

I stopped my make-up repair and faced her. "It felt like you couldn't say no to him?"

"Yeah. That is what I wanted to tell you. I felt like I was compelled to be with him and couldn't say no. Like I was under a spell. Now, I think I know why. But I wanted to tell you; I didn't mean to do it. We've gone through so much in college together. I'd never steal your man. Rich was yours when you first told me back in that Chem course. He wasn't for sharing. I'd never go against my word. Please believe me." She leaned in closer and whispered in my ear. "After all, I know you're witches now, and I didn't realize that when you found us. I figured now you'd understand."

"You know Rich and I are witches, and you're good with that?" I whispered back. I eyed her suspiciously as she nodded. He'd have trouble holding the spell now if she knew.

She leaned back, looking me in the eyes. "Yeah, but I haven't done anything with him since. He said it would be good to try to find you here, and maybe tell you everything."

"I know Rich can be real convincing." Witches knew it wasn't cool to use spells like that on mortals. Cassandra wouldn't know that. "It was a shitty thing to do to me, even for him."

"So, you believe me?"

I nodded. Somehow, she seemed sincere in her pain. Rich could be convincing even without spells. A mortal he wanted would have no resistance. "At least this tells me one thing. He didn't want to stay together anymore. Why else would he spell you into bed?"

She reached over and gave me a hug. I hardened up. I wasn't sure if I was totally forgiving her yet. But she started to creep into my arms and relaxed. She seemed to radiate the need for forgiveness. It chiselled at my resolve. Besides, I had Jeff now. Rich could fuck anything he wanted at this point. I said finally, "Okay. I forgive you."

"See. Forgiving solves half the man problems in the world." We both turned to the attendant. "Now you're half way there, honey." I couldn't help it, but laughed hard.

"Someone should pay you by the hour."

"They do, but it's never enough."

I smiled and pulled out a twenty and placed it in her tip bucket. "It was worth the advice to get a friend back."

"He slept with your friend. He's worse than a rat. Friends are worth more than men any day."

I grabbed Cassandra's hand. "You can say that again. I'm glad I can see him for the bastard he is." Forgetting about fixing the rest of my make-up, I dragged Cassandra back to the bar where Jeff stood. His stunned look spoke volumes.

"Guess who I found?" I looked at Cassandra and she nodded back.

# Chapter 4

"So I wanted to apologize after Rich chased you out of your mansion, and he suggested we try to find you."

The three of us sat at the bar, Jeff and I listening intently to Cassandra's side of the story. "So, we drove north at first. Then, he stopped and we turned toward Vegas."

"Must have been after we met him at the diner." Jeff's voice sounded strained.

"No, I was with him the whole time. We spent a few days going north, and then turned to Las Vegas. I couldn't figure out where we were going."

"Neither could I." I smiled at the thought of my wanderings up Highway 1 before picking up Jeff as a hitchhiker, strange how things could turn out.

"Then, before you know it, we were staying at the Aria, and we went next store for drinks at the Chandelier. And there you were with another man. I thought, well, maybe this is good. She'll understand now."

"Are you thinking what I'm thinking?" Jeff perked up when Cassandra's mumbling story got to the part about meeting up at the Chandelier.

"Not sure." I was busy listening to Cassandra's mutterings, trying to read her for honesty. Rich was a conniving bastard. How could he try to separate Cassandra and me? She was my first mortal confidante.

"She's bait, Cat."

Both Cassandra and I turned toward him.

"How so?"

"Were you upset to see her last night?"

"Yes."

"And how would her being here still affect you? Or is it still affecting you now?"

I looked at her, and I thought of what an asshole Rich was to spell my best friend against me. "It would make me mad. But I don't think he's counted on girlfriend power being stronger than him." I clinked glasses with Cassandra.

"But how do you feel with her here?" Jeff eyed me, waiting for my answer. That might not have been good.

"I'm even more pissed off at him."

"Would you be reasonable right now?"

"Not really. If he came through the door right now, I might blast his ass."

"Exactly. It's his typical strategy. Throw the woman off balance, and you've got her. You need to control your emotions. Remember what I said about being patient? He won't expect you to be calm. I don't think many witches are."

"It is hard to be calm around warlocks, Jeff." He gave me a funny look. "Sorry. But Cass and I have been through a lot together. Using her like that was a low blow."

"Exactly again. He might have been planning this for a while. It might be part of his strategy. If you are weakened emotionally, he can separate you from reason, and win. And what would he get in the end?"

I thought for a moment. "The house, the car. Wait. My inheritance. Damn it." I took another drink. "Shit. He's probably been planning this for a while."

"And if he was after your money in the first place, this would be the final step."

Cassandra grabbed my hand. "God, Cat, I'm sorry about this. I would never have introduced you two if I'd known he was such an asshole."

"It's okay. It's hard to believe I let myself fall for him so hard, and not see all this." I rubbed my forehead. I was starting to get a headache.

"I think that was the point, Cat. You fell hard, and he thinks he's winning. Let us keep him thinking that." He turned to Cassandra. "It might be too dangerous for you to go back to him. He would be able to mind spell you and see you've made up with Cat. It would be bad for you then, I'm afraid."

I could see Cassandra draw an anxious breath after his comment. I put my hand on hers. "He's right. I think you're going to have to stay with us for a while, until this is over."

"What's over?"

I looked at Jeff and then continued, "The spell battle. It's how witches get divorced."

"Shit." Cassandra took a sip from her glass. "I didn't know. I just wanted to come here and apologize, Cat. I didn't want all this to happen. It's all my fault." She started to cry, and I pivoted on the barstool to lean forward.

"No. It's Rich's fault. This is worse than I thought. And I'm glad my eyes are wide open now. Who knows what would have happened if I kept running? I got to talk to you. Now I know. It's all him. I should have thought of that earlier. But I did get a bit distracted." I nodded over to Jeff.

She snuffled and wiped her nose with her hand. "Yeah. He's the best distraction anybody would want. Seriously. You are so strong, Cat. You always were."

"I keep telling myself that. Now you have to be, too. I still have to face Rich. With you here, it poses problems."

"It's probably what he wanted, Cat," Jeff interrupted.

"Yeah, I'd be off balance no matter what happened with Cassandra here. What do we do?"

Jeff put his hand on mine. "Beat him at his own game. Put him off balance."

"But how do we do that?"

"Leave that to me." He smiled, and I saw a glint of mischief fill his eyes. I've got an old score to settle. It's time for me to call it."

"Are you going to tell me what the plan is?" I noted his playful glimmer again. He was up to something.

He smiled and took a sip of his drink. "Nope. Won't work then. But I do have an idea. Why don't you and Cassandra get caught up? Go do something."

I looked at her. "You thinking what I'm thinking?"

She nodded, and we clasped hands saying the word we lived for, "Shopping."

\*\*\*

"Hold on, Cat, I've got to put these bags down for a second."

Damn, I'd forgotten the limited shopping stamina of mortals. We'd had a chance to go back to our rooms and rest. It was an endless night of talking and catching up. Now we were off early, shopping our hearts out in the Forum Shops at Caesar's Palace. It was almost like Rich was a bad dream. Nothing like a little make-up shopping to put a friendship right again. "'Kay. Let's take a break at one of the restaurants. You hungry?"

"I could use a coffee." Cassandra let the bags she was holding lower to the floor.

"Right. Let's head over to the Cheesecake Factory. It must be about time for lunch."

"Sounds good to me."

I picked up Cassandra's other bag, and we headed in the direction of the restaurant. It was good to be out shopping with Cass again. I didn't know how much I'd missed her until we were trying on shoes at Michael Kors. What's a friend to do without her shopping buddy?

We got into line for a table and gave our names. I flashed a move-around spell to inch us further on the roster. Meanwhile, I breathed in the sweet aromas that filled the restaurant. Between the sweet smell of basil, pasta, and Brie, I was going to swoon. My stomach gave a rumble as if on cue.

"Banks."

"Right here." I waved down the maître d', and he began to seat us as my witch radar went off. I felt a scan spell coming from behind. Turning would have been a bad move. It would have alerted the spell caster. I kept a steady pace behind Cass and the waiter, and when we arrived at the booth, I sat facing what I thought was the direction of the spell, so I could look around.

Nothing. I didn't see anyone, which meant it had to be a strong witch. Damn. Maybe Cassandra was being missed.

Rich wouldn't be that crazy to get close to me this soon. We couldn't blow up Caesar's Palace. Too noticeable, not to mention already having been done in the '80s. A couple of witch battles had been covered up with demolitions.

"You look kind of creeped out, Cat. Something wrong?"

"I don't know." I lay down my bags next to me in the booth. "Seems like we're being watched."

"You can tell?" She leaned forward trying to keep her voice down.
"A spell was cast to scan us. Not sure who yet. Just pick out something to eat. I'll try to scan back and see if I hit something."

As Cassandra looked over her menu, I used mine, with a flip of my hand, to set the spell. It was a subtle enough spell that it wouldn't trip the dampers. Most of those centered near the casinos. Besides, witches felt out each other's energies all the time. But I had to be careful.

The spell swept the room, taking my mind into each corner. There. Someone in the left corner. A dark shadow. I sent an exposure spell in that direction, and there was a flash to my witch eyes. A dark figure stood up and glided out. It wasn't human. But it had been following us.

"Damn. I hope Rich isn't sending reinforcements to check on us. But it wouldn't be unlike him."

"Something popped up?" Cassandra lowered her menu.

"No. Go back to looking. You want to seem natural. It wasn't human. It could be a watchdog trying to see what happened to you. If anything, we might have lost the surprise element. Rich must know we've talked."

"But will he know anything else?"

"Well, we're shopping. And you're still here. That means that he knows we've talked and made up."

"Is that good or bad?"

I smiled. "It's good for me, Cassandra. Friends are better than any warlock. We couldn't let one, especially one as bad as Rich, stand between us. It just took me some time to realize it."

The worry that crossed her face relaxed. Her eyebrows returned to normal as she went back to her menu.

'That's what I wanted to hear. The guilt has been killing me. Sorry, I'm such a bad friend."

"No. You're not. It wasn't your fault. You showed me how much of an asshole Rich really is. I totally blame him. I can see that now."

I put the menu down and grabbed her hand. "Besides, I missed you. The last couple of days, I've had a lot of ups and downs. I could use a real friend again."

"It means a lot that you forgive me, Cat."

"I know. Funny thing is, I think I need it, too."

At that moment, the waiter came and interrupted us for our order, always on cue. But I was ready to eat now. In fact, I was ravenous. Something inside me had clicked. Rich cheating on me had been bothering me, but the fact that he'd chosen Cassandra had hurt the most. It was as if something had clicked in my mind, and all of my hostility could focus on him. Maybe I was sharpening my witch tools. Revenge could be sweet. The question was what was I going to blast off first.

When the food arrived, I got lost in the taste of chai basil chicken pasta and an amazing tropical iced tea. My problems were temporarily forgotten thanks to my food infusion. In my rush, there was a by-product I couldn't hide. I burped.

"Wow, that was explosive." Cassandra's lips wrapped around the straw with a smile as she sucked down her soda.

"Well, better out than in."

"I missed this."

"Me, too."

We held up our glasses and clinked. I got back to devouring my pasta when I felt a sweep behind me. My instincts put up a shield as I stopped eating.

"Something wrong?" Cassandra stopped with her fork midway to her mouth.

"I just felt another probe with a spell. Something is definitely watching us. I'm afraid, this might end our shopping spree."

Cassandra smiled. "But at least we got to get shoes at Michael Kors."

I laughed. "Totally. Mission accomplished. We're supposed to meet up with Jeff soon in the hotel, anyway. At least I'm going to savor this pasta. I've so earned it."

Of course, I was hoping we wouldn't bring our tag-along. Something was definitely watching. I kept eating to hide I was on to it. I extended my shield over Cassandra, and I felt the mind sweep fade. Deciding to chance it, I turned and looked behind me. There was no one there.

The booth was empty. I stared into the emptiness, feeling the tinge of something undead. Swirls of blackness tried to enter me. I flipped my hand into a block spell, and it dissipated. I did a skim of the restaurant to make sure whatever it was had completely left. If anything, it was leaving trails, and that meant I could follow it.

"Come on, Cass, we've got to get out of here," I said as I got a few twenties out to leave on the table.

She looked at me and wiped her mouth. "Sure, whatever you say."

We grabbed our bags and wove through the people in the aisle and out into the Forum shops. I did another sweep to see if I could pick up its trail. I felt the dark energy surging out of the shops and onto the Strip. We left the Forum and walked across the ramps and steps that led into a garden below. Under the rays of the desert sun, the garden of statues and plants created a Roman oasis. But I felt the trail of dark energy going over the street bridge to Bally's and Harrah's across the street.

We joined the press of people, sweaty and laden with purchases. Going out during the day in Vegas was not high on my list of options, but whatever I was following could wander in the daylight. That gave me some idea of what it was.

We were going down the escalator when I spotted the dark shadow moving in Bally's, and we followed, if for no other reason than I'd welcome the air conditioning. We pushed our way through the Bally's/Harrah's square, trying to make our way through throngs of shoppers and tourists so I could catch a glimpse of what had pursued us.

I doubted that any mortals could see the shape moving between them. It took on different shapes as it eased through the spaces in the crowd. Some people backed away from the areas it eased through. There was only one thing that I could think of that could take a form like that. Black Ooze was one of the best spy familiars that could tail a witch. It had been subtle, too. I'd been distracted by Cassandra. She was taking me off my guard. I had to focus.

I was literally dragging Cassandra through the crowd until we finally reached Harrah's casino door. The clanking of slot machines assaulted my ears as the blast of cold air hit us through the entrance. I was losing sight of the shadow. It was going through the machines faster than I could drag Cassandra. I could leave her and double back, but I didn't want to chance leaving her alone. This was the first time a mortal felt as heavy as a stone.

"Cat, I don't think I can keep up this pace." She slowed, pulling back from me.

"We're going to lose it, Cass. I know that you can't see it, but it's ahead of us in the crowd."

"Go after it, Cat. I'll wait here. I'm in the casino. There are tons of cameras. I'll wait here by the roulette tables."

I could see the shadow ahead and said, "All right. Don't move. I want to see who it's going back to report to. They don't have much range."

"'Kay." She stopped in the aisle, leaning against a slot machine, and took off her shoes to rub her feet.

I gave her shoulder a quick squeeze and blasted off after the thing at witch speed. It seemed to realize that I was going faster, since it started taking more zigs and zags through the back part of the casino. My shoes started to slip on the marble floor, and I had to veer onto the rug to avoid a spill.

We were nearing the back of the casino, near the parking garage. I caught the last glimpse as it turned down a hall near the elevators. Then I lost it. Damn.

I figured it could have gone through the wall, but Black Ooze needs a crack for that. Not good if there are cracks in the walls for any casino. But it could have gone to the back rooms. I circled back through to the casino, to the machines and roulette table where Cassandra had been standing. She was gone.

"SHIT." I did a circle spin, as people took a moment to wonder about my angst. But this was Vegas. People didn't bat much of an eyelash for my concern for Cassandra. I sent out a wave of power, searching, creeping through the casino and out on the nearby streets. Gone. She was nowhere nearby.

At that point, I knew it was a set-up, and I'd fallen for it. I stood outside Harrah's, hands on hips, and made a resolution. It was time to stop thinking of a strategy, and come up with a plan. I knew Rich was behind it. And hopefully, our standoff would be soon. I was feeling anxious for the battle. My fingers twitched with energy. I think it was what I'd been running from all this time. Rich. It was time to face him.

# Chapter 5

The only thing I could think of was going to see Jeff. He was back in our rooms. When I made it through the door of our suite, it all came out in a rush. "I lost her."

"Shit. Cat, what happened?" He put his arms on my shoulders, and I did some dry heaves before I calmed down enough to let him know the whole story. When I was finished, he wiped a tear from my cheek. Damn. He really was impressive sometimes.

"It had to be a set-up. She's your weakest point. He's going for your area of vulnerability. It's going to undo you if you let it."

I snuffled. I couldn't help it. Rich had put me through so much. Now he'd taken Cassandra from me a second time. I couldn't let this bastard keep getting to me.

"I've got to face him, Jeff." He held me closer as I started to let it all out. "Which means there's going to be a battle."

"You sure you want to go through with this?"

I nodded as he held me closer. "I have to face this. I've got to face him. He's ruining my life at every turn now. I want to be in charge again." He lifted my chin and gave me the softest of kisses. I melted into his embrace. "Will you stand next to me? I need you as my pillar to lean on."

His answer was a kiss that drew me into his arms further. I got lost in that kiss. His lips sipped at each of mine, pulling them into his mouth, with just enough suction to pull at my soul. I started to wrap a leg around him using it to draw him closer. He couldn't take it anymore. He picked me up and threw me on the bed.

"For now, I want you to forget about facing Rich. I want you to think about us."

He started taking off my T-shirt, lifting it over my head. I got up on my knees and matched his balance on the bed. I took off his shirt. I glided my fingertips down his chest. Goosebumps rose on his skin as my finger traced the front of his chest. I stroked up and down his midriff, making him shiver.

He started to moan slightly, and I took the lead. He leaned back on the bed as I started to crawl over him. "Do you think you need these any more?" I reached for his belt to unbuckle, then began to unzip his jeans, slowly.

"Careful not to get things caught," he mentioned as I continued unzipping.

"When am I not careful?"

He sat up, but I pushed him back down. "Let me do the work now. I'm in charge."

He let me pull off his jeans. I stood up on the bed, undoing each button of my jeans. I peeled off each leg, and threw them over my shoulder onto the floor. I unhooked my bra and let it fall on him. He grabbed the bra and tossed it onto the lamp.

I fell down upon him, gliding over him as I kissed along his whole chest down to his underwear. I got to his briefs and started to slide them off.

"No, with your teeth."

"Oh, you are a bad boy."

I kissed his stomach and moved to hover on the edge of his waistband. I took the elastic in my teeth and pulled down. There was a shudder that moved through him. I grabbed more of a mouth full and gave a good yank. Then, matching my pull on the other side of his briefs, I used my hand to slide them down as much as I could.

"Um," spitting out bits of fluff, "this might take awhile."

"You got all night."

I looked at him feeling like the Cheshire cat. "That I do. I hope you're patient."

I grabbed another hunk of his briefs, and moved them a bit further. Inch by inch, I made progress until, "Oh hell. Fuck it."

I grabbed the sides of his briefs and pulled. His cock flopped out hard and erect.

"There might be one more thing to do now."

I eyed him as I said, "Now it's your turn. Teeth only."

He grabbed me and flipped me so I was under him. He took the edge of my panties with a growl. The roughness of his teeth caressed my skin as he switched from side to side, clearly having done this before. The wetness grew between my legs as I felt him move between my inner thighs. He threw my panties and aimed at the lamp. They missed and hit the wall.

"You don't get any points for that."

He leaned over me and hushed me with a kiss, pulling on my lips, teasing me, and caressing my stomach. I eased my legs open, inviting him, urging him to enter me, but he held himself back. Instead, he used his rod to tickle my clit, sending mini shockwaves through my groin.

I pulled his hand away and enveloped the length of his shaft within my warm, wet folds, as I slid back and forth, building us both into a frenzy. Then, slowly, teasing in his thrusts, he began to enter me. Tender at first, and then a slow push. He'd pull out and watch my face.

"Don't make me beg, Jeff." I leaned up to him, pawing his chest to continue. "I need all of you. In me. Now."

I reached my hands around his firm butt and pulled him into me. He thrust again and again until I was unable to think about anything but him. The passion and desire was more than I'd expected to feel. It was what I needed tonight. It was what I needed...

"Jeff," I whispered.

"Yes."

"I so need you."

"I need you, too."

"We're one, joined as souls."

"Forever."

Then I didn't think about anything as we gave over ourselves into the bliss of our love. We were one. Forever.

# Chapter 6

I woke in his arms. The sunshades on the windows weren't pulled down, and the sunlight made the room glow. I tried to shield my eyes as they adjusted. I slipped on my robe and walked out into the living room. As I looked out from our suite on the twenty-sixth floor, the Strip lay out below me, shining under the desert sun. Pools glinted back, with whole open areas dedicated to sun worship. I looked out at the expanse of Las Vegas trying not to think of what I would do to Rich.

The one thing I knew was that Cassandra was going to be a pawn in all of this. I had to not let it be so. And I didn't know how to stop it.

I heard Jeff open the bedroom door and walk up behind me at the window. He wrapped his arms around me.

"What are you thinking?"

"Wondering where they are."

He nuzzled me closer. His nose went through my hair caressing my neck. "Try not to think of them. You're here with me. Try to think of the here and now."

"Okay." I turned in his arms and leaned into his chest, letting him envelop me with his arms. There was this. Jeff. Us. That's what I had to think about and focus on, and not let Rich endanger this.

"I think I'm ready to face him," I whispered into his chest.

"I'm ready to stand with you. All I have to do is call Tristan, and he'll arrange the show down."

"I wish I didn't have to."

"There's another way, you know." I looked up into his eyes as he said, "We can get married. Instead of your vows being returned, you say new vows. It would end your arrangement."

Tears slowly welled in my eyes. Here it was. One warlock or another. I leaned into Jeff, feeling his breathing, his arms tightening around me. He held me close as I searched within myself. Was I ready for another warlock? Or did I need to stand-alone?

I breathed in deep. Jeff waited, holding me, as I started to cry. "I want to move on."

I stepped back from his embrace and reached up to hold his face in both hands. "Will you marry me?"

He answered with a kiss that smothered all of my arguments against being with him the rest of my life. He was the ship in my sea. I could climb upon him and feel safe forever. He gave me one word. It's all I needed. "Yes."

I had a thought that made me pull away slightly. "The question is when?"

"The answer is pretty easy. It could be right now."

I couldn't help but laugh. "You're right. But where can we book a chapel that quickly."

"There's the drive-through."

I snorted. "Well, even I have to draw the line there. A girl needs a little drama on her wedding day. With the right spells, we should be able to set up something before my vow deadline today. But where?"

"I'll make some phone calls. How about, you go look for a dress?"

"Now you're talking." I was feeling better already. Shopping would put me in a better mood. "I know one thing. Buying a new dress always improves a woman's attitude… toward anything. Especially a wedding dress."

"Get ready then." He turned me toward the bedroom and gave me a pat on the butt. "You've got shopping to do. I'll call Tristan and ask for his help finding somewhere for us to get hitched."

I flared with excitement. "See you in a bit. I bet I know the perfect place downstairs for a dress." I'd been eyeing a gown in the window along the Venetian Grand Canal shops. It could be the one if it fit. "We've got several hours before the deadline of my vows with Rich." My heart swelled when I saw Jeff move toward the phone, his bare-chested body full of purpose. I sealed the image in my mind forever. No matter what happened, we had each other.

I dashed to get dressed, threw on a skirt and blouse, and ran back for a hug from Jeff. He was on the phone talking to one of the chapels, and he gave me a big kiss in mid-sentence. I could hear the person on the other end of the phone calling out, "Hello?"

"Sorry, got distracted there for a second," he said to the woman, then turned back to me. "Okay, off with you." He swatted me on the butt again. "Go get a knock-out dress."

I gave him a wink and dashed out the door.

\*\*\*

I ran toward the elevator filled with excitement. It carried me through the casino. I was overdosed on the high of love. A wedding-dress shopping-spree feeling took me over. I glided through the great hall of Renaissance murals mounted across the ceilings.

I walked through the entrance into the Canal Shops and followed the echoes of people and water. The great hollow sound of the enclosed shops on marble floors made it unique in all the Vegas shops. I was heading to the shop where I'd seen the gown in the window. It was off-white, with beadwork worthy of the Oscars' Red Carpet. I stood in front of it, looking the dress over, imagining the sweep of the beadwork over my shoulders, the lace curving around my hips and legs. It was a top-notch designer. And it had to be mine.

I swept into the store and found the sales lady coming at me with the Vegas attention to detail. Before she could ask, I was turning toward the dress in the window. "I think that might be my wedding dress."

The sales girl lit up with my comment. "When's the wedding?"

"Today. I'd like to try it right now, please."

She went over and took the mannequin down to undress it. "I'll bring it back in just a moment." It was an eternity of looking at the other dresses on the racks as I waited for her to retrieve the dress. But I did hover over accessories. I was going to need some sparkle if I was having a Vegas wedding. God, I liked the sound of that. Could I get an Elvis impersonator to preside? A girl could dream. My mind was running on overload just as the sales girl came out with the dress.

It was better off the mannequin. It was cream-colored beadwork all around the edge with a slender cut. It was something that screamed Marilyn Monroe in GENTLEMEN PREFER BLONDES. It looked like what I'd imagine for my wedding. The fact I was in Vegas was a bonus.

"Here, let's get you trying this on." The sales girl broke my reverie as she guided me to the dressing room. "Would you like some assistance?" she asked as she showed me to the door. I shook my head and reached for the dress, too excited to speak. She handed it to me and said, "Be sure to let me know if you need my help. I'll be outside the door."

As I slid into the dress, I could tell by the feel that it fit perfectly. I didn't even have to cast a spell to alter the dress. I took this as a good sign. It slipped effortlessly around my hips, and the beads dripped on either side of me. If I did a shake, the beads swung in little clicks around me. I took a look in the mirror. I felt like I was glowing.

"If you need some alterations, I think I can put a rush on it."

I stepped out of the dressing room to get a look in the full-length, three-way mirror.

"Oh, girl, I think you'll be fine. It's a perfect fit."

I looked in the mirror and saw myself as a bride. Well, a Vegas bride. I think I'd turn heads walking down the street.

"Do you have anything to go with the dress yet?" she asked.

"No. I knew this would be the dress as soon as I saw it, but I still need some shoes, and a necklace to set this all off."

"Leave it to me. I think our private shopper can help you with that."

Before I knew it, she was on the phone calling someone down to help piece my wedding outfit together. I love how things can get solved with phone calls in this town.

A woman entered the store ten minutes later, just as I had gotten out of the dress and handed it over to the sales girl who put it on a hanger and was slipping a garment bag over it. "Where is our bride to be?"

"Right here." I raised my hand, feeling like a schoolgirl.

"Hi, I'm Phyllis." She offered her hand as I gave it a gentle shake. "How much time do we have?"

"I'm guessing we have until three p.m."

"Wow. That is quick."

"I've got a rather important deadline. I've got to be married again by four p.m."

"Then, we'll get you ready, darling." She had a southern lilt to her voice, and a '60s retro hairdo. "First things first. You need shoes, a matching necklace, and earrings. May I see the dress?" I nodded as she slipped it out of the bag. "Good color to match most anything. Do you like sparkle?"

"Oh God, yes."

"Then, I think I know the place." After I paid for the dress, Phyllis whisked me off to a jewellery store with an exclusive Swarovski crystal selection and helped me pick out a necklace and earrings. From there, we headed to the shoe store and got some outrageous heels studded with sparkles. I was definitely going to be a shining bride. If nothing else, I could always stab Rich with my shoes. My train of thought was distracted as Phyllis led me into a lingerie shop.

"The most important accessory for any bride is the lingerie. Men love taking it all off." Phyllis had a partner in crime grin as she helped me pick out a matching bra, panties, and an old-fashioned pair of stockings with seams down the back. I held up the garter belt. It had ribbons of blue woven in the white lace. It had been a while since I'd worn such a thing.

"This makes everything sexy, but proper for a wedding." Her southern lilt accented the word "proper," and I had to hold back a laugh. I was anything but that. If only she knew what I'd been up to a few nights before. I couldn't wear white for this wedding, but no one had to know that.

I returned to our room with my bundle of wedding essentials, prepared for the epic battle that would determine my future. Whether I lived or died, it would be at Jeff's side.

He was still on the phone when I walked in. "It's like nothing changed while I was gone."

"But everything has changed." Jeff walked up to me with a big grin. "I've set up a ceremony at the Little Chapel on Las Vegas Boulevard. All the arrangements have been made. Best of all, Elvis will be picking us up."

I dropped my bags and threw my arms around him. "It's like you read my mind."

"Well, I kind of did. Our soul bond was so strong, I couldn't miss the images of Elvis singing and performing our ceremony."

I gave him the biggest kiss, and he returned it with equal passion. "It's the perfect Vegas wedding."

"For the perfect Vegas bride."

"You didn't peek into my mind and see the dress?"

"I might have caught a glimpse or two, but not the full effect. If we hurry, we can make the lunch reservations downstairs. That will give us time to change before Elvis picks us up."

"I think I love you."

"I hope so. We're getting married."

At that, the laughter drove us downstairs to meet our fate that afternoon. Whether it was facing Rich or vows, it was going to happen. Four p.m. was the deadline for destiny. I had to run facing it, or at least die trying. Standing with Elvis, in a fabulous, beaded designer gown, standing by the man I'd fallen in love with was the best way to meet any destiny.

# Chapter 7

I was dressed to the hilt. My hair was up and heels sparkled as I walked. The beads on my dress were glimmering in the lights of the Venetian lobby. I was feeling ready to get hitched. All we needed was Elvis to pick us up and take us to the chapel. The doorman gave a whistle as he held open the door with a grand arm flourish.

As I walked out of the hotel, I saw a fabulous pink '50s convertible Cadillac pull up. Eyeing the convertible, I was glad I'd put my hair up. But I needed one more thing. I stroked my hair, sending a spell into my upsweep so it would hold with the coming assault of wind. The tingling over my head told me the spell had taken hold. It could survive in a wind tunnel now.

Behind the wheel was young Elvis. He was complete in a black shirt and pants with his classic Elvis up sweep hairstyle. His dark sunglasses added to the mystique. I made my way to the car. Somehow, I wished I'd brought my sunglasses. People were pulling out their phones to take pictures. It wasn't everyday Elvis drove up in a pink Caddy.

"Are you ready?" Jeff asked as he grabbed my arm and opened the door for me to get in.

"Hell, yeah."

We settled onto the leather seats as Elvis pulled out onto the Strip. Classic Elvis tunes blasted on the stereo as our Elvis impersonator asked if we needed water to start our journey. Most mortals would be melting in the heat, but I took the bottle in case. Taking a sip, I looked around as people stopped on the street watching us go by with Elvis driving. This was definitely the way to be driven to our wedding. But just in case, I was keeping an eye out for Rich. It was three-thirty p.m. Anything could still happen.

Then it hit me. I was going to my wedding. I guess I was nervous. Needing to relax, I let the voice of Elvis wash over me, leaned back in the leather seats, and took a sip of water.

"You seem like a great couple. Congratulations on your wedding day." Elvis had the perfect tone of the original. So much so, it was going to make me cry. This was turning into my Vegas dream wedding.

"Thank you. This is one special day for us , " I answered as I took another sip to keep a waterfall of tears from starting.

Elvis looked into the rear view mirror. "It takes meeting the right person. Looks like you got that. You both lean back and relax. I'll get you to the chapel on time." He winked, making me laugh. He was right. I took a deeper breath as Jeff wrapped his arm around me.

We stopped at a light, and I got a good look at the people doing double takes from the crosswalk. Elvis driving a pink Cadillac is something you may expect in Vegas, but probably not what you saw everyday. I was excited to be in the middle of it. It was helping me forget what might await me at the chapel.

We passed the Stratosphere and continued down Las Vegas Boulevard to the downtown area where wedding chapel after wedding chapel started to appear on either side of us. We passed the infamous pawnshop from the TV show PAWN STARS and turned right shortly after into the parking lot for a small white chapel. We got more stares from people waiting for their moment in the chapel. The party before us was posing for pictures and getting ready for their moment.

For full effect, Elvis walked around and opened the door for us. Jeff got out first, then turned and reached for my hand to help me out. "We have to check in with the wedding coordinator."

As he held my hand, my excitement started to bubble over. We were really doing this. We were going to take the vows that would end this nightmare with Rich. We entered the air-conditioned reception area, and a woman quickly checked us in, handed me a flower arrangement from a refrigerator behind her desk, and showed us the paperwork to fill out.

Jeff filled in the forms as I took a look around the lobby. The chapel stood along the street with a few buildings lined up behind it. The check-in lobby and a photo studio were in the back. The rest was a parking lot.

There was a small grassy area where people stood in line waiting for their turn to enter the chapel. As a group moved into the chapel, the receptionist directed us to take our turn on the grass. I plopped down on the wooden bench. My feet needed a rest.

Elvis was the only one in our wedding party, but he was definitely the one to have. I was starting to wish Cassandra was here, and put the idea of her standing at my side firmly out of my mind. I was sure Rich would be up to something, and I had to stay alert. Damn. If he was going to strike, it would be now. It felt like the closing of an adventure, and I still didn't know the ending.

I stood up and brushed off the dress to get the beads to hang straight down.

Elvis came over with his own bottle of water and after a sip asked, "So, where are you both from?"

"Sydney," Jeff answered keeping alert, as well. He seemed to feel this was the time Rich would attack, too.

"Northern California," I answered drinking water, as well. Even for witches, the desert air sucked up any moisture when you were outside. Wanting to get my mind off of things, I changed the subject to distract my mind, but stayed alert. "What kind of Caddie is that?"

Elvis nodded. "That's one of only two still around. It used to belong to Lucille Ball. I take good care of her."

I piped in, "As well you should. Classic cars are like people. Each is unique. Truly one of a kind."

"Especially this one," continued Elvis. "I've had some pretty impressive offers, but I won't part with her. She's my baby."

Feeling impatient, but knowing it might have to do with fireballs flying through the air at any time, I asked Jeff, "When is our appointment time?"

"Three forty-five. We're going in next."

It was three forty p.m. I had five more minutes to back out and run like hell back to the Strip. This was indecision time, but as I looked back at Jeff, he seemed to see my anxious face.

"It will be okay. We've got this. You and I are already one, remember?" He held me with his gaze for a long moment.

I nodded, still apprehensive. How was I to know whether that was true? Then, I knew the answer. I wasn't. I wasn't sure of anything. All I had was Jeff saying it was true. If I believed him, I could believe in our future. I could say our vows and seal our vow for the next year, together forever if we chose from now on.

A man in a suit came out of the chapel doors. "It's time."

"Are you ready?" Jeff had the cutest expectant look on his face.

I reached for his hand and gave it a squeeze. "Yes. Let's do this."

We followed the suited gentleman into a waiting area, as he motioned for Elvis to follow him. Elvis turned to us. "I've got to go set up. Listen for my singing for your cue to walk down the aisle. I'll see you both in a moment."

Elvis made his way into the chapel. Another woman motioned for us to take a position near the door. We spent the next few minutes looking at and holding each other. The giggles started as the woman opened the door for us to walk down the aisle. Rose petals were lying about on the floor. They were most likely from the last wedding, but they gave a little added charm to our moment. We were sharing in an ancient custom of binding two lives together. It felt right we were sharing it with others today.

We heard the perfect imitation of Elvis's voice starting the song, "I Can't Help Falling In Love." At that point, we started moving down the aisle, hands joined, with the sound of Elvis singing, our lives starting anew as we journeyed together toward him. He had added a gold lamé jacket to his wardrobe for the ceremony, collar up, of course. He looked like he'd just walked off of the Ed Sullivan show.

Tears started to well, and I held them back, if only to keep the moment solid. I wanted to do this full hearted, without totally losing it. If Jeff was to be mine, I needed to do it with a totally clear head. We stopped in front of Elvis, his smile moving from Jeff to me.

"We are gathered to witness the joining of two people. People who cared enough to share this moment of wedlock in the place that does it best, Las Vegas." He gestured to the chapel and continued. "For this is not an easy thing to decide, but to be taken greatly and seriously as two souls join into one. The vows must be true and honest, or all is for not. You do understand this, don't you, Cat?"

I had been looking into Jeff's eyes, but this didn't seem right. I looked back at Elvis. "What are you talking about?"

"All must be right for the vows. It must be heartfelt." At that point, the glamour fell, and Rich stood before us, still dressed as Elvis, but with a horrible sneer across his face. "You can choose between us. Are you going to renew your vows with me, or choose him?"

I think Jeff and I instinctively threw up our shields, because Rich sent a jolt at us both that almost knocked us down.

"You've always been good at glamours, Rich." Jeff was the angriest that I'd seen him.

"And you've always fallen for them, Jeff. It is your weak point. Oh wait, I forget. You have another weakness."

Rich raised his hand and waved it on the right side of the chapel. A woman appeared bound and gagged in the front pew. Her eyes widened, and whines broke through the cloth in her mouth. Blonde hair and blue eyes were dead-on ringers for Jeff's. I could see the Elvis impersonator also bound and gagged in the chair next to her. His sunglasses had been knocked off, and his eyes burned hatred toward Rich.

"I know this isn't the best way to meet your possible future sister-in-law, Cat. But it seemed appropriate for the occasion." Rich waved his other hand to the left side of the chapel and Cassandra appeared. She was bound and gagged, but rage filled her eyes. If allowed, I think she would have bitten off pieces of Rich, too.

"Really, Rich. That's your move?" The sarcasm dripped from my speech. All this was just getting me angrier. I couldn't help myself. "Hostages? Like some bad TV movie. I must say, I expected more. Even some kind of wooing move. A last attempt to seduce me would have been more effective."

Rich had the look of already being the winner. He folded his arms. "No, I think a choice is best, Cat. Choose their lives over ours together. Come back to me, or they die. It's simple. Their blood will be on your hands if you don't."

"So you're telling me that if I don't choose you, you would actually kill them?" I snorted. "Rich, you were never creative with revenge." I could see Jeff easing back, slowly approaching his sister. I could tell he was following my lead. If we could get close to everyone Rich had bound, maybe we could shield them. Then bang, I felt Rich's counter spell hit me as I tried to shield Cass on my side.

"Nice try. You probably felt the backlash of how I've spell-locked them from you. Nothing can release them but your commitment to renew our vows together."

I smiled. Jeff said to be patient. I was starting to see the wisdom of his words. If the spell was timed, maybe it would end at four p.m., our vow renewal time. If I was patient and waited him out, maybe. I just had to be patient.

I took a deep breath. Slow and steady. "So, I have the choice of continuing a farce of a marriage with you or death for my friends and in-law to be?"

I just had to get Rich to play along a little longer. "How can I be assured you will really let them go?" I had to think back to all timed spells. An action whether it was the intended or not, would happen at the time set. I figured if Rich was thinking he was winning, he'd let the time spell play out. Then after, it was up to me.

"Well, Rich, I must admit, I've missed you all this time." I started to ease up next to him, stroking his chest through the black shirt. I'd felt the curves so many times, I knew exactly where one of his turn-on spots was and started working my hands that direction, using the deft touch I knew he responded to. "I've talked to Cass about it, too. If Cass and I could make up, maybe you and I could, too?" I let my eyebrows go up on the "you and I" to emphasize my suggestion.

I left it hanging in the air, and didn't look at Jeff. I felt the spark of passion between Rich and me ignite for a moment. The marriage bond was still there, and his bad-boy body and attitude were turning me on. I let it zing through my body so Rich would believe the moment and hopefully feel the link between us. Maybe he'd believe me.

Then, I heard a crushing sigh come from behind me from Jeff. He must have felt it, too. Rich grabbed me around the waist, claiming his victory. "You lose again, buddy. I always get the girl."

I knew I couldn't look at Jeff's face. I was going to have to do this on my own, if I was going to convince Rich. My shield was protecting me, but I was wondering if I could shield my soul-crushing guilt. I had to play this right, or it wouldn't work.

"I'm sorry, Jeff. Maybe I just like the bad boys better than the good." I tried to sound convincing, and it came out vicious. "Too bad, though. I was really enjoying our playtime together. But I guess it's really you I have you to thank. You taught me patience. I knew it was only a matter of time before Rich and I were together again."

His startled look could have been taken for shock at what I said. But I felt our soul bond strengthen. Jeff's next words to Rich told me he understood. He'd heard my clue. "Rich, I know I've only beaten you once. It was probably because it was my sister, not another woman. You always got the women in college, buddy. You always had the badass touch. Anyway, it's Catherine's choice." He let his shoulders sag. Sighing deeply, he went to hold his sister. You could hear the gong of the time spell breaking, as both she and Cassandra were released.

Rich tightened his hold on me. "It's time, babe. Let's say those vows."

"Absolutely. After all, it's my choice."

At that moment, Jeff and I snapped protective shields around Cassandra and Jeff's sister. Then I turned toward Jeff and shouted the traditional witch's marriage vow: "For one year for here I stand, I take the warlock of choice in hand."

I ran to Jeff as he ran to me. Rich's force spell bounced off our shields as I grabbed Jeff's hand to finish the vow. "This vow I say heart felt and free, to be with you for a year's eternity. So mote it be."

An electric charge filled the air and sparks flared between Jeff and me as we bonded. Jeff shouted his answer to seal the vow, "I agree to fulfill this vow. For one year to be, her warlock for one year's eternity. So mote it be."

The boom echoed through the chapel and startled some of the mortals in the sound booth and the one at the piano. But knowing Rich, I grabbed Jeff's hand and Cassandra's, knowing he'd grab his sister, and we started to run. I knew what happened when one crossed a warlock. Things usually exploded. Running was the safest thing to do.

As we exited, fireballs began to fly our way, but it was the chapel itself that took the heavy damage. The walls blew outward, and we dove for cover behind a grassy mound as debris flew over us and bounced off our shields. I could see people running away from the building, including the real Elvis impersonator, hands still behind his back, heading our way and taking a dive for cover.

At the last minute, I extended our shield to cover the pink Caddy next to us. Then it hit me. I hopped into the car, extended my hand and shield to keep debris from landing on the car and the others by the knoll. "Come on." I waved for them to join me.

The others didn't need to be told twice to jump in the car with me. More parts of the chapel building flew outward as more fireballs hit the lobby and photo studio. It was turning into a war zone.

I sent a spell into the motor to start it and backed out race car style onto the boulevard. My shield kept the pieces of chapel from landing on us as we escaped the downpour. I looked in the rearview mirror to see the small chapel completely engulfed in fire. People were off to the side watching it burn. In the distance, I heard sirens coming toward us.

I made a U-turn to flip direction back toward the Strip. I floored the Caddy, urging all the speed I could out of the ol' girl as we flew back down Las Vegas Boulevard. Cass ended up next to me, with Jeff in the back. Jeff's sister was next to him, being held by the Elvis impersonator. I assumed Jeff must have spelled away his restraints.

"Well, that was some wedding." Cass chirped as the wind whipped her hair.

"Only in Vegas," Jeff said as he reached out his hand for a high-five with Elvis.

I smiled. I finally felt free. My journey ended with a new start. Looking in the rearview mirror at Jeff, I knew it was the right direction. "Shit yeah. Only in Vegas."

## Acknowledgments

Every writing project is an adventure. I'd like to thank those that have brought me to this point in my journey. To my husband, you are my human cat. Thank you for making me purr when I need it the most. To my beta readers that give it to me straight, Lisa Frogjourney and Lady Trish, thank you. I'll remember to refrain from giving my characters blue balls in the future. To my editor Shelley Holloway, thank you for the polish you give all of my work. You make it all shiny. Your encouragement keeps me going and in the panic moments, "Don't worry, it's fixable" can limit my meltdowns.

Most of all, I'd like to thank my readers. All of your comments have helped shape the Beware of Warlocks series into so much more than I first thought possible. Thank you for loving my characters as much as I do. They are living, breathing aspects of what I see or have experienced. To have you all enjoy my books makes it all worthwhile.

I will endeavor to keep my nose to the grindstone and churn out more adventures for Catherine and her friends. There is a whole underground world of witches evolving in my mind, and it's centered in Vegas, baby. Plus, a new series is in the works for her friend Cassandra called Beware of Vampires. Be sure to check out my website for more information and sign up for my newsletter. Thank you to all my readers for being a part of my writing journey.

For the latest information about new releases, promos, or just tell me how you felt about this omnibus edition, visit my website at: http://marilynvix.com.

Newsletter Link: http://eepurl.com/MWT2L

Find Marilyn Vix on social media at:

Facebook: https://www.facebook.com/marilyn.vix

Twitter: https://twitter.com/MarilynVix

Pinterest: https://www.pinterest.com/marilynvix/